THE HAUNTINGS OF THISTLEBRAE FARM

BOOK ONE
A RACE WITH TIME

Rosie Ann Stewart

Paperback Edition 2021

ISBN: 978-1-9160857-1-8

CONTENTS

ACKNOWLEDGMENTS

To my family for being so patient and encouraging me to get this finished, especially my daughter Michelle. She spent hours assisting me with developing some of my characters and going through the story aloud to make sure everything flowed and made sense.

Thank you to my Grandson Ethan who helped me with some of the technical stuff and kept me sane when I was trying to put my book on Amazon.

A special Thank you to Marie Thompson for illustrating my book cover

INTRODUCTION

The old house was waiting patiently for new lives to come into it. Soon they would come and everything would begin again.

It was empty now and had been for many years, though it was never alone. There were occupants, lots of them and most of them children. Some friendly and some not so friendly. Some family and some were enemies. They too were waiting, though not so patiently.

Would they win this time or would the curse claim more lives? Would they end up with yet more playmates, or would these new children manage to solve the mystery and break the curse forever? Only time would tell and time was something the young ghosts had plenty of. Unfortunately, the new children would not be so lucky.

The ghosts knew that their new family would be one of their own. They knew that the new family would be McGregors and there would be more than one child. The family had never visited the house yet and probably was unaware of its existence, but they would very soon.

The ghost children would make very sure of that. Meanwhile they would keep an eye on the other ghosts who were getting restless. They did not like the house being disturbed and had decided to have a little fun with the workmen who had been hired by the Estate Agent to renovate the house. Trouble was coming.

HOUSE HUNTING

It was a hot summer's day; the sky was blue with no clouds to be seen. The sun was shining brightly in the sky. The date was July 3rd and it was the last day of the school term. The children were excited. The summer holidays were almost here. How could anyone be expected to concentrate on activities inside the classroom when all of them, including the teachers, longed to be outside enjoying the summer sunshine?

Nicholas and Katie, although just as excited as everyone else, also felt a little sad. Today was their last day at primary school. After the summer holidays were over, they would begin high school at the local academy. Although not identical, as one was a boy and the other a girl, the twelve-year-old twins were very much alike. Both had dark brown hair, brown eyes and freckles in the same place across their nose. Each had a dimple in their cheeks when they smiled or laughed. One twin usually knew what the other was thinking and when one started a sentence the other would usually finish it.

However, there were some differences. Nicholas would usually act first and think later of the consequences of his actions, whereas Katie would think through a problem first and then take action. As a result of this it was usually Nicholas who got into trouble and Katie who got him out of it. Where

Nick was practical, impulsive at times, funny and he had a way with animals, Katie was headstrong, sensible and the decision maker.

Their brother Christopher had an inquisitive and enquiring nature. He loved computers and anything to do with technology. He was the one who would take things apart and rebuild them just to see how it worked.

Michelle the youngest of the family was the most sensitive of them all. They had all been told by their Aunt who was a well-known Psychic and ran a school for the psychically gifted, that Michelle had been born with certain gifts and would one day be as good a psychic as her aunt. So far her abilities had not shown themselves other than by being very sensitive to atmospheres and sometimes having premonitions.

The twins attended the small country school along with their younger brother Christopher aged ten and their nine-year-old sister Michelle. All the McGregor children were especially excited because not only was it the beginning of the summer holidays but also today was to be an extra special day. Their parents were collecting them from school and they were all going to look for a new house.

Their mum and dad, Mary and James McGregor had decided that now that the children were growing older and there would soon be two new additions to their family, it was time to move to a larger house with more space. Mr. McGregor was a Farmer and he was looking for a farm with a little more land so that he could expand his business. He was intending to rent out his present farm to his brother Brian who was also a farmer but had just returned home after several years living abroad.

At last lunchtime came. Some tearful good-byes were said with plans to meet up sometimes during the holidays and then school was finally officially over for the summer. As the children ran out into the summer sunshine their teachers breathed sighs of relief. Now they too would soon be free for a few weeks. There would be a break from having to plan lessons or having to maintain discipline in the classroom or even having to correct piles of homework in the evenings.

Outside Mr. and Mrs. McGregor were waiting patiently in their blue land rover. They too were excited. After all it was not every day they went looking for a new house. As the children happily greeted their parents and made their selves comfortable in the car they were very excited. "Where are we going to visit first Dad?" asked an inquisitive Nicholas.

"We have two places to see this afternoon and another one to see tomorrow morning." His father replied. "The first one is quite close to town and I am not at all sure that it will suit us. I would prefer a little more land." His father went on to explain. "The second house sounds more promising. It is bigger with more land and very cheap for its size. Of course, it will need work done to it, as it has been a few years since it was last occupied and it depends on the soil type. I have it on good authority though that it is good fertile land. The third house is a newer house with only slightly more land than we have just now. The present owners are going to live abroad. Unfortunately, it is further away so you will all have to change school."

Hearing the groans from his children and before they could start complaining he quickly continued. "However, the beauty of the first two houses is that none of you will need to change school. Both the houses we are looking at today are in the school catchment area so if we decide on one of these two you will not have to lose any of your friends." Dad finished, feeling very pleased with himself.

"What! You mean there won't be any new nice-looking boys for me to meet? Oh, no! I don't like the sound of this at all." Katie moaned disgustedly.

"Boy crazy Katie!" Michelle taunted her sister.

"So, what's the matter with that? You're just jealous because you can't get yourself a boyfriend." Katie taunted her sister back.

"I can so. I'm just fussy who I choose. Besides you will be starting a new school so there will be new boys." Michelle shouted back. She was beginning to lose her temper now.

"Oh yes! I forgot about that." Katie smiled.

"Okay that is enough you two, just calm down now. Here we are at the first house so I want you all on your best behaviour." warned their mother.

As both the houses they were to look at that day were unoccupied, the estate agent had given them the keys to both the houses so that they could take their own time to look around the properties. As he

would be seeing them the following day he would collect the keys from them then. He would also find out then if any of the properties would be suitable for them.

The first house turned out to be a disappointment. The bedrooms were very small and the kitchen was tiny. The barns were in a state of collapse. Everyone felt quite disappointed. “Funny it looked much bigger on the website.” Mum said disappointingly.

“Yes, and it didn’t look so run down either in the photos. There is far too much to do to get the land ready for planting and for the animals that will be coming with us to move straight away.” Dad replied a little frustrated. “What a waste of time”.

The second house however was a different story. The children loved it, all except Michelle. There was something about the house that did not feel right to her. She was a very sensitive little girl and could sense things that her brothers and sister could not.

This house gave her the creeps and she kept getting cold shivers down her spine. She knew that there was something bad lurking in the house somewhere. She could feel it. She could feel the hair at the back of her neck prickling. It made her feel quite frightened. "I don't like it," she complained to her mum. "There's something about it. I don't know what it is but it’s scary. I feel like I’m being watched all the time. It feels really weird and it’s so creepy it’s giving me goose bumps and shivers all over."

"Nonsense!" Her Mum tried to calm her daughter.

"The house is old and needs work done to it. It is not scary. Most of the windows are boarded up and both the house and the garden have been neglected for quite a while. There is nothing here which cannot be fixed." She said trying to be cheerful. "Let's go and see what it's like inside." She knew that her younger daughter was not very keen to go inside the large farm house.

The outside of the house had looked scary enough for Michelle, but she dutifully followed her parent inside. Mrs. McGregor gave a sigh of relief. She knew that Michelle was not as keen as the rest of the family to move. After all she had lived in their present home for the whole of her young life.

Mrs. McGregor worried about her youngest daughter sometimes. She appeared so young and fragile compared to her older brothers and sister. With her long curly auburn hair and freckles, she didn't even look like the other children. Her father often teased her that someone had switched her with the real McGregor baby in the hospital just after she was born. Of course, that had stopped when her husband's mother had shown them some photos of long dead family relatives. The family resemblance was very strong in Michelle.

Unfortunately, it wasn't the resemblance to long dead family members that caused her to worry. It was something else that she had inherited from her dead ancestors, from both sides of the family tree Michelle seemed to possess at times an almost uncanny psychic ability. She was worried how these abilities would manifest themselves. Her husband's brother Brian also had these gifts which he had inherited from his Grandmother Annie who had been gifted.

Mrs. McGregor sighed again. Her own Aunt was a very gifted and well-known psychic too. She smiled now as she remembered that it was due to both these ladies that she had met her husband. The two ladies had met at a spiritualist meeting and had immediately become friends. Unknown to either herself or her future husband the two friends had set the pair up to meet. Again Mrs. McGregor smiled at the memory of her first meeting. Her Aunt had invited her to stay with her for a short time. During her visit, her Aunt had persuaded her niece that she was feeling unwell and would be unable to visit her friend as arranged. Her friend would feel very let down and disappointed. She had then persuaded her niece to go in her place.

Her friend had been staying with her Grandson on his farm. Once there old Mrs. McGregor had suddenly become very tired and had gone to lie down leaving her Grandson to entertain their guest. The rest was history. It was at their wedding that the two ladies had come clean about their meeting claiming that it was in the stars that they should meet and fall in love. They had only given destiny a helping hand.

Mrs. McGregor was very grateful for their helping hand. She loved her husband very much. What she wasn't so grateful for were the psychic genes that her youngest child was giving every indication of having inherited from them.

Sometimes her daughter could sense things before they had even happened. Mrs. McGregor shivered as she remembered a time about a year ago, when she had been two and a half months pregnant. Michelle had had a bad dream and woke up crying. She refused to tell her about the dream at the time but had found out later when it was all over. For a whole week after having the dream, Michelle had been sad and had cried a few times. She had kept giving her Mum cuddles and saying that she was sorry. A week after the nightmare Mrs. McGregor had found out that she had lost her baby. The baby had been dead for about a week.

She touched her tummy and prayed that it would not happen again, as she entered the house. She was heavily pregnant with twins this time. She was tired and she just wanted the move to be over with so that she could relax and get things prepared for the babies arriving.

It was a large very old period house that had been added to over the years. Surprisingly inside it looked to be in quite a good state of repair, considering that it had been unoccupied for so long. It had been owned by a trust that had decided to sell it off. However, it did look more than a little gloomy. The rooms were large with plenty of cupboard space. There were small dark gloomy looking side corridors. In some rooms, the windows were still boarded up. The small amount of light coming through the slats in the boards were casting strange and sometimes frightening shadows. The older children thought this was great, but they didn't wander too far from their parents.

The kitchen came as a surprise to them all. Unlike the other rooms this room was light and airy. It was a very large kitchen with a large walk in pantry. There was a utility room which led off from the kitchen which in turn led to a boot /cloakroom complete with shower. This would be ideal for the dogs and the children and their father coming in with their messy muddy boots.

In the kitchen, it was obvious that some work had been carried out very recently. New work surfaces and cupboards had been newly fitted. An aga cooking range had been installed. It was a lovely kitchen, just how a farmhouse kitchen should look like. Mrs. McGregor took one look at the red and white colour scheme and instantly fell in love. The work surfaces and units were red, the aga coking range was red and there was even a normal cooker which was red too. By the two windows there were two window seats. The walls and the beams were a newly painted white. Mrs. McGregor was already planning what she would do. White table and chairs would fit in here very well. She would recover the seat covers with a red and white spotted material; make new window seat cushion covers and curtains all in the same material. Her fingers itched to get started. Her mind was made up. This was it. This was the house she wanted.

Mr. McGregor was also impressed with the house, but also a little mystified. The kitchen was unfinished. Some of the cupboards still needed doors attached to them. The doors with their fastenings and screws lay on the work top ready to fix. The workmen had obviously not finished the work yet. They had left their tools behind. A half-finished sandwich and almost a full cup of tea lay on a newly finished worktop. A newspaper lay untidily on the floor as if someone had been in the middle of reading it and then all of a sudden had hurriedly flung it down. From the way that the tools and everything else had been left, it all looked as if the workmen had left in a great hurry. Mr. McGregor made a mental note to himself to ask the estate agent about it when he saw him the next day.

The rest of the house was just as impressive although it was a little gloomy and very cold in places. There was also an unpleasant musty smell in some areas of the house. Mr. McGregor had checked for any signs of dampness but could find none. On their tour of the house they noticed other disquieting signs of the workmen having left in a hurry. It was obvious from their observations that a central heating system had been in the process of being installed. Of the workmen, there was no sign of them. The house proved a hit with Mr. McGregor he couldn't wait to get outside to look over the outside buildings and the all-important land. The house would be useless without the land.

They spent the next hour looking over the land and outbuildings. Although the barns needed some work done to them they did not need much to bring them to standard. The work could be done quite quickly. The land was good and he had taken some samples for testing the soil. It all looked really promising. He was very optimistic that this was the one. He could tell his wife was becoming tired so they made their way back to the house.

"Well what do you think kids?" Mr. McGregor asked his children.

"It's great, Dad. There are so many barns and outbuildings here too can we have one for a games room? Maybe we can have the one next to that big oak tree near the house?" Nicholas asked his Dad hopefully.

"Yes, that would make a great games room." Chris agreed.

"No not that barn I didn't like it." Katie said quickly. "There was something about it."

"You sound just like Michelle!" Chris was annoyed with his sister. He didn't want to ruin their chances of getting a great games room of their very own.

Mr. McGregor sensing another argument was on the way quickly repeated his question. " Can we buy it? Please can we?" chorused the three oldest children.

"I don't like it." Michelle moaned. "It's creepy and smelly."

"That's only just now Honey." Michelle's father tried to reassure her. "Once it has been painted and decorated and we have aired the place and once the workmen have finished the work which has been started, the house will have a whole new atmosphere."

Mr. McGregor was as excited as his three elder children were. He could not believe that such a desirable property was going so cheaply. Having completed a quick tour of the property, both inside and outside he had discovered for himself that there was good potential farmland here. The property contained more barns than on his present land. Amazingly most of the barns were in good weatherproof condition. He was eager to start work on the house too. Already he could picture in his mind the changes he would make to the place once he started to decorate. Yes, he thought to himself, he would be a mug to pass on this place.

Mr. McGregor was not the only one who found the place impressive looking; his wife too liked what she saw. She was very much impressed, though she did have a few reservations. She could understand her daughter's comment about the place being creepy. Never the less she was sure that once the place had been properly decorated and with the house carpeted and furnished, the atmosphere of the place would seem much friendlier and much less creepy. She was six months pregnant with another set of twins and did not want to spend all summer long house hunting. If they bought this place, then everything could be ready by the time the babies were due to be born. Mrs. McGregor looked at her husband, he looked at her then they both nodded simultaneously and smiled. It was decided. This would become their new home.

Christopher who had witnessed the exchange of looks between his parents gave a shout of joy. "Great, we're gonna buy this house. This is gonna be our new house. Bags I get the room at the top." He grabbed his brother by the hands and they both danced around the room.

Only Michelle was unhappy about her parents' decision to buy the house. "I don't like it. I don't like it I tell you." She shouted angrily. There is something that just isn't right about the place. It's evil," she moaned.

."Rubbish!" Christopher scoffed. He looked at Michelle, paused and then laughed wickedly. "Unless you think it could be haunted? Ooooh!" he taunted his little sister. He was at that age when boys could be quite unwittingly cruel towards those younger and more vulnerable than them.

Michelle did not react in the way he expected. Looking him straight in the eyes, Michelle gave her brother a very strange look. "That's just it. I think maybe you're right, maybe it is haunted." Michelle replied softly, a little nervously and very, very seriously.

The house was silent. Everyone had gone. In the kitchen two ghost children were sitting at the table discussing the visit. They knew that this was the family who would be moving in. So, who do you think we should approach first?" The little ghost boy asked. "The little girl has some awareness. She seemed to sense us."

"Yes, but she is very young. We might scare her. Maybe it would be better if we choose one of the older ones. Her older sister might be the better one to approach?"

"You forget how young I was. There isn't much time so it is important to get them helping and trusting us quickly."

"Yes." The girl agreed. "I forgot how young you and your brother were. We should approach her gently so as not to scare her. I hope her brothers and sister believe her. The first meeting must be carefully planned."

"If they don't believe her we will make them believe. Let's go find the others." The little boy laughed as they floated away.

Chapter Two

THE FIRST ENCOUNTER

The following day, Mr. McGregor and his sons returned to the farm. Before committing himself into buying the farm he needed to be very sure that this was the property. He arranged for a building surveyor to examine the buildings on the property, including the house, to see exactly what work would have to be carried out. He also wanted a closer look at the land and was meeting his Farm Manager and Supervisor at the property to get their input on whether the land was suitable for farming and keeping animals on. The boys wanted to tag along because they wanted another look at everything, especially the barn they had earmarked for themselves. Their sisters had not chosen to go with them. Katie was unhappy at the choice of barn her brothers had opted for and Michelle well she was just unhappy with the whole property choice.

After spending all morning at the farm Mr. and Mrs. McGregor visited the estate agents who were responsible for dealing with the sale of Thistlebrae Farm. From then on everything seemed to happen quite quickly and in hardly any time at all the McGregor family were moving into their new home.

In fact, it had only taken a month from their first visit to the farm. It had taken that amount of time to complete the alterations to the house. The estate agent had explained that the workmen who had been working on the house had had a disagreement and had walked out. He then explained that new workers had already been hired and were due to begin work the next day. Mr. McGregor had felt that Mr. Moffat, the estate agent had been keeping something from them. He had been nervous whilst explaining the situation to them. However, he had let it pass without comment. Had he known what the Estate Agent wasn't telling them he may have thought twice about buying the property.

Mr. Moffat the Estate Agent had spoken with the workmen who had left the job so quickly and had been unable to believe his ears at what he had been told. He had of course heard the rumors about the place being haunted but had never believed it till now. However, as he really did not want the property hanging around on his books like a millstone for the rest of his life and he really wanted the sale, not to mention the sizable commission he would get on the sale of the property, he kept what had happened to the first group of workmen to himself. He had no intention of frightening his potential buyers out of the sale.

The workmen had reported hearing strange noises in the house. Doors were opening and being banged shut for no reason. A couple of them had reported seeing dark shadows coming towards them and footsteps on the stairs. Lights flickered off and on all the time. The last straw which had scared them all into running away, frightened out their wits and convincing them once and for all that the house was haunted, came when they were having their lunch break in the kitchen.

The workmen all heard noises in the hall and footsteps running. The main door to the house was shut. There was no one else in the house. The running came closer and then suddenly the kitchen door flew open then banged shut. The temperature in the room dropped and suddenly the air was so cold they could see each breath they took. Cupboard doors opened and shut so quickly it was like a gust of wind blowing through the kitchen. The workmen were terrified. One workman felt his arm being tugged and stood up with a scream then, when he felt his arm being released; he quickly sat back down and landed on the floor onto his bottom with a thud. A ghostly laugh was then heard. This was enough for them and they dropped whatever they had in their hands, cups of tea, sandwiches, and the newspaper as they all pushed past each other to run out the kitchen, along the corridor and out the door never to go back. They could hear the sound of ghostly laughter echoing through the corridor as they ran.

Mr. McGregor had then hired a firm of decorators to carry out the decoration work needed in the house. Everything went very smoothly and finally it was moving day and they were moving into their new home. The children were sad to be leaving their old home but very excited about moving into the new house. Apart from Michelle who had thrown more than one tantrum during the past month. She had tried everything she could from coaxing, to threatening to move to her Grandparents, and finally to tantrums to try to change her parents' minds about the house. Her parents were adamant. They would be moving to the new farm and so was she.

On arriving at the new house, the four children were sent outside to explore so that they would not get underfoot of the adults who were busy unpacking. "What do you think of our haunted house now Michelle?" Christopher laughingly teased his sister.

"I still don't like it and I'll bet you it really is haunted. Just you wait and see, then we'll see who's laughing." she replied seriously. The other children just laughed and acted as if they were ghosts to try to frighten Michelle. Unlike their sensitive little sister they did not believe in ghosts. Humphing with frustration she stormed away for a walk on her own.

Michelle intended on going back to the house but felt herself being drawn towards a clump of trees in the distance. She didn't want to go in that direction but it was as if an unknown force was compelling her to go there. She tried to stop and turn but her feet would not cooperate. She felt her hand being taken. She was being led to the trees by someone or something. A calm feeling came over her. She should have been terrified but she wasn't. She felt calm, relaxed and for some strange reason, happy. She also felt safe, knowing instinctively that whoever or whatever had her by the hand guiding her would not harm her. They wanted her to see something.

Quite soon she came to the clump of trees. In the middle of the trees she walked into a clearing. Once in the clearing she found a wooden bridge over a small stream flowing into a small pond. It was a lovely quiet place and Michelle found it delightful. There were wild flowers and an old wooden bench and in a far corner of the clearing was an old swing. Michelle thought that the place would be ideal for a picnic area if her Dad was to paint the bench, renew the swing and add a picnic table. Michelle felt her hand being released as she walked across to the swing. She gave it a small push to test if it was safe. It was obviously a very old swing and unused for quite some time as it was rather creaky. Luckily the swing had been made to last and though creaky it was still quite strong.

It was whilst she was having a swing on it that she first saw the vision. Michelle was feeling quite tired. She had been late in bed the night before and had been up very early that morning. The swinging motion of the swing kept making her nod off to sleep. Therefore, when she saw what she did see, she was not unduly alarmed. She just thought that she was having a dream. Everything seemed to take place whilst she was in this hazy, dreamlike state. Later she was to wonder if this had been deliberate so that she would be more relaxed and receptive.

On a bench at the opposite side of the pond an old woman sat knitting. On the ground by her feet a young girl of about eight years old was playing with a doll. At one side of the bench there was an old-fashioned perambulator. [That is a pram to you and me.] Inside the pram was a small boy. He looked to be about only eighteen months old. He was lying kicking his feet and sucking his thumb. The little girl stood up. She was dressed just like a young Victorian girl, wearing a long white pinafore over a long dark blue dress. The girl turned towards the swing and slowly advanced so that eventually she came to stand directly in front of Michelle. The girl smiled. It was a very sad smile. She reminded Michelle of someone but could not remember who that person was. Just as she opened her mouth to speak, there was a sudden noise from the direction of the trees.

Michelle blinked and looked towards the trees and then back again to the Victorian dressed girl, but by then the little girl was running back towards the old woman. She turned to take a last quick look at Michelle. She looked a little frightened. Just then Michelle heard someone shouting her name. Her brothers and sister must have come looking for her.

A few moments later Katie, Nicholas and Christopher came walking into the clearing. There was no longer any sign of the old woman, the girl or of the baby. There was just the empty bench. Everything appeared and felt normal now and Michelle was wide awake.

"Look at this place, isn't it brilliant? Trust you to find it first Michelle." Katie exclaimed as she looked around her excitedly.

"Did you see the girl and the old woman with the baby? Did they pass you? They were just here too." Michelle asked a little puzzled.

"What? We never passed anyone. You've been sleeping and dreamt it, I'll bet." Nicholas answered mockingly.

"No." Christopher interrupted him laughingly. "She's been seeing those ghosts that she keeps talking about."

"Ha! Ha! Very funny." Michelle replied rudely, giving her brother a filthy look. She shook her head and rubbed her eyes. "I must have dreamt it, but it did feel real."

She came down off the swing and was about to move away when she spotted something shiny on the ground in front of the swing. She bent down and picked it up. It was the small cameo brooch, which she had seen the little Victorian girl wearing.

"What is that you've found?" Katie asked coming to pear over her sister's shoulder to have a look.

"Look! See! I wasn't dreaming. They were real, I did see ghosts and this proves it. Look it's the brooch which the girl was wearing." Michelle answered a little dazedly holding out the brooch to show the others.

As they all gathered round to look at the brooch, Michelle recounted what she had seen before the others had interrupted. "Wow! A real ghost!" Nicholas said enviously. "Not even one but three and all at the same time. Lucky you!"

Christopher was more skeptical. "What makes you so sure that they were ghosts? It could have been people dressed up just to scare you. We didn't see anyone so the brooch must have been lying there on the ground for a long time. Admit it you dreamt it all. You don't want to move here so you are just trying to scare us. Well you won't put a damper on things. I like this place and so do Nick and Katie so just get over it. Anyway, we're here now so nothing you can do about it. We've moved now. It's too late! As from today we live here so just get used to it" Chris finished angrily. He had been expecting some back up from his elder brother and sister and was surprised at how gullible they were.

Both his sisters threw him withering looks. "If that's what you think, then why didn't you see them as you came down the path?" Michelle shouted angrily. "All three of you came down the path. They couldn't have gone any other way except the way you all came. They just vanished. One minute they were here the next they were gone. Besides Look! The brooch is clean and shiny. If it had been lying on the ground in the dirt for any length of time it would be dirty and rusty. Look at it does it look dirty and rusty? They just have to have been ghosts." She said determinedly.

"I wonder if there are any ghosts up in the house." Nicholas interrupted quickly putting an end to their squabbling. "Maybe you'll see them again. What

are you going to do with the brooch Michelle? Are you going to tell mum and dad?"
"I don't know. Do you think I should? They probably won't believe me. You know what grown-ups are like. For all they know I could of just found the brooch." Michelle replied seriously to her brother's query.
"Well personally I don't think that we should say anything to the parents. It would only worry them, even if they don't believe us." Katie said wisely.

It was agreed between the four of them that nothing would be said to anyone else. It would remain their secret until, and only if, they could provide absolute proof that there were ghosts on the farm. "After all," Nicholas told his siblings, "It could just have been a fluke, a one-off experience never to be repeated." [Oh how wrong he was.]

The children decided to look around to see if they could find any more clues. Once again Michelle was made to tell them everything, which she had seen and heard in exact detail. After all, they had reasoned with her, maybe she would remember some small but important detail that she had forgotten before. Something, which could maybe, give some vital clue as to the identity of the girl.

It was as Michelle was telling them again about how the girl had been about to speak to her that she had heard them shouting to her from the woods.
"She looked quite frightened. The noise you all made must have startled her. It must have been then that she dropped the brooch. "
"But Michelle, we never made any noise in the woods." Katie interrupted excitedly.

"We were going to sneak up on you and give you a fright. We were really, really quiet."
"You couldn't have been. You shouted my name. You did, I heard you." Michelle accused her sister.
"We did not. I swear to you Michelle, we didn't. Guide's honour, we did not shout on you. None of us did." Katie defended them all.
"Well someone shouted my name, unless of course," Michelle pondered slowly.
"Someone could have been shouting on the girl. Maybe her name is Michelle just like me."
"Maybe it is someone who lived on the farm before us. In the past maybe" Katie suggested. "Maybe we could carry out an internet search on one of those ancestor sites".
"We can't cos we don't know her name". Chris reminded her.

He was still very skeptical but had decided he would humour them as Michelle really believed it and she didn't lie. He was a kind boy and loved his sister so in order not to antagonize or hurt her he would play along with them for now he thought.
"Hmm! Well maybe we could carry out a search on the farm on the net to see what we can find out. Once the internet is up and running". Nick suggested.

The others agreed and on the way back to the house Michelle was a lot happier. She was finally being taken seriously.

When Michelle was giving her mother a helping hand to put her clothes away in her room her brothers and sister got together to discuss their sister's experience that morning.

Christopher was still a little angry with his brother and sister for being so gullible. However when they told him that they had not really believed her and had just been humoring her after all, he was even more puzzled. Why would they do that? Katie explained that as their sister had truly believed what had happened it would give her something to focus on and stop her moping about. "Besides," Katie added. "You never know she might be right. If Auntie Winnie is correct then Michelle has inherited the family Psychic abilities. If she is right it could be fun".

In another part of the house there was another meeting going on between the ghost inhabitants. They were happy with the first meeting and how receptive the little girl had been. What they were not so happy with was that although the others had told their sister they believed her, they had lied.
"The younger boy could be trouble. He clearly does not believe his sister". The little ghost boy said.
"No, he does not, but neither do the other two. I think they are pretending to believe her to keep her happy". The little ghost girl replied. She felt quite frustrated that they had not believed their sister.
"So, what are we going to do about it? Another visit to the little girl do you think? It's a pity they don't believe her because one of them is in for a big shock. I can only hope it isn't the little girl." The ghost boy asked.
"Yes, another visit with more evidence to show them that they have to believe her. They will believe though and soon. What is this internet they spoke about? Is it some kind of book do you think?"
"Maybe but they won't need that." A second older ghost boy laughed. "We will make sure of that. Our

book has all the information they will need." The others laughed with him

"Yes, but we must get them to read it first. How will we get them to do that?" The little ghost girl asked worriedly.

Chapter Three

MICHELLE'S MIDNIGHT VISITOR

Their first week at Thistlebrae Farm was very busy. The children spent their time unpacking and setting up their rooms how they wanted them. They helped their mother unpack her ornaments and kitchen equipment. In their spare time, they explored the house and the barns and outbuildings surrounding the house. This took some time as the old house had many nooks and crannies. Next, they explored more of the grounds coming across some exciting places and old buildings.

There had been one barn that three of the children had particularly enjoyed exploring. Their Father had promised to make over one of the out buildings as a games room for them. The children had taken one look in the old small barn and had earmarked the building as their games room. Katie was the only one who had not been excited. For some reason, which even she could not explain she had taken an instant dislike of the place and had refused to even enter it. Whilst her brothers and sister had fun exploring the barn she helped her mother in the house.

The old barn seemed to be in good repair but as it had not been used for many years was dirty and dusty. The children loved it and came home grubby but happy and full of plans on how they wanted their games room to look. Much to their amazement Katie was not amused. "You are all crazy! Dad hasn't even said you can have that barn yet. He will probably need it for the cows or something."

Her twin was frustrated with her and more than a little puzzled. This wasn't like her. Normally she would be the first person with the plans and would be as excited as the rest of them were. "It is too small for the cows and Dad did say we could have it, just not yet. What is with you Sis? You are sounding just like Michelle." He shook his head still very puzzled especially when he received no come back answer from Katie.

They were waiting, impatiently at times, on their telephone and sky lines getting installed so they could set up their computers, ipads and mobile phones to the internet. In fact, it was so busy that the children almost forgot all about Michelle's encounter with the little 'ghost' girl. However, the ghosts were not willing to let this state of affairs last much longer. They were also growing impatient.

One night about one week after their arrival, Michelle was wakened up by the sound of someone crying. She sat up in bed and was about to reach out to turn on her bedside lamp when she changed her mind. Her eyes slowly became adjusted to the darkness of the room. It was not so very dark as there was a full moon that night and Michelle had not closed her curtains. She could see quite clearly the little girl from the pond.

Michelle swallowed painfully. Now that she knew the little girl was a ghost, she was a little scared. Why did she have to be the one to keep seeing ghosts? Why did she have to be the psychic person? Wasn't it enough that their Aunt was very psychic? She asked herself. What should she do? However, she could see that the poor girl looked very unhappy. Michelle's kind and sympathetic nature soon overcame her fears. She seemed to know instinctively that this ghost would not harm her in any way. In fact, the little ghost girl looked so innocent and defenseless and appeared to be very upset about something.

Plucking up her courage she looked at the little ghost girl, "What's the matter? Why are you crying? Is there something I can do to help you?" Michelle asked a little nervously. At first the other girl did not seem to hear Michelle's questions, so she asked again more confidently. This time the little ghost girl appeared quite startled. She jumped and quickly turned around to look at Michelle. She stared at her for a moment then as if making up her mind about something, slowly approached the bed.

Michelle's fear of the unknown was mirrored in the eyes of the little ghost girl' "Why she is as scared of me as I am of her." Michelle thought. "If she appears as a ghost to me, I wonder what I appear to be to her." Just then the little ghost girl spoke. "Wh... Who are you?" she stammered nervously. Michelle answered her softly and soothingly, trying to calm the little girl's fears. "My name is Michelle and I live here with my parents, my two brothers and my sister. Who are you and why are you here? You've been crying. Is there something I can help you with?" she asked gently.

"Oh! How strange! I too am named Michelle. I live here too with my baby brother, our nursemaid and my guardian. I have seen you before have I not? It was down by the pool. You were on the swing. I think perhaps that may be where I have lost my brooch. My Uncle Jamie who is my guardian has discovered its loss and is quite annoyed with me. It was my Mother's brooch and he gave it to me on the understanding that I would take the greatest of care with it. He demands me to recover it and I know not what to do." The little ghost girl began to cry softly to herself again.

"Don't cry, oh please don't upset yourself. There is no need to. Honestly there isn't." Michelle tried to calm and soothe the girl. "I have your brooch. I found it by the swing where you must have dropped it. It's in my jewelry box. Wait here and I will fetch it for you."

Michelle jumped out from her bed, went across to her dressing table and took the cameo brooch from her jewelry box. She walked across to the other girl and held out the brooch. "It's a lovely brooch. I'm not surprised that you are so upset at the thought that it might have been lost." Michelle admired the brooch as she handed it across to the waiting girl. She was much more confident now and not scared at all.

Unfortunately, giving the brooch back to the little ghost girl proved not to be too easy. The little ghost girl try as she might, could not pick up the brooch from Michelle's hand. Michelle then tried to drop it into the other girl's hand but with no success. The brooch just went through the hand to drop on to the floor. Their efforts would have been funny to watch and both girls would probably have had a good laugh together if the matter had not been so serious. "Perhaps if I put the brooch down on the bed or better still leave it down on the floor, maybe you can pick it up from there. After all when I found it, I picked it up from the ground." Michelle finally suggested. Luckily Michelle's idea worked and the little ghost girl was once again reunited with her mother's brooch. She smiled with relief. Michelle smiled back.

The following morning Michelle woke up late, just as her sister Katie was entering her bedroom.

"Come on sleepy head. Dad is taking us all on a picnic today and you haven't even had your breakfast yet alone done all your chores for the day. Come on, hurry up the sooner you get up and get everything done then the sooner we can all leave."

Michelle just yawned and stretched lazily. "You know, I had the strangest dream. I dreamt that I saw that ghost girl again. Do you remember the girl down by the pond? Well she was in my room last night. She was crying because she had lost her brooch, so I gave it back to her and then we... Oh! Wait a minute, I wonder...." She stopped talking for a moment and then suddenly jumped out of bed, went across to her jewelry box and searched through it. "Oh! Wow! It wasn't a dream after all. It was all true, it really did happen".

"What really happened? Katie was confused and a little frustrated with her sister. She wanted her to hurry up and get dressed but she was being annoyingly slow. She wanted to go on the picnic but Michelle appeared to be in no rush and talking in riddles. "Talk sense Michelle! What are you talking about for goodness sake? Stop talking and hurry up and get dressed!" She shouted.

Michelle tried to dress quickly as she spoke excitedly to her sister. "Sorry I forgot you wouldn't know." Michelle apologized and quickly told her sister all that had taken place during that midnight visit. "We had a wee talk afterwards. Do you know that her mother was French and her father was a Scottish Laird? They all lived here until her parents suddenly disappeared one night. No one knows what happened to them and they were never seen or heard from again. It's such a shame! I feel so sorry for her. Anyway, afterwards she lived here with her Uncle who was her guardian. The woman I saw at the pool was her nursemaid and the baby was her brother. She said that her guardian is kind to her but is very strict and hasn't much time for her, so she is very unhappy and you'll never guess what Katie! This girl is also called Michelle McGregor. Her Dad was called Donald McGregor and her uncle's name was Jamie McGregor. I wonder if they are related to us in any way. This Michelle says that she has what she calls 'visions'. She has met people from the past and from the future too. Well," She clarified, "that is from her future but from our past. Her visions are of other children who have all lived in this house at one time or another. Isn't that strange?" She finished.

Katie stared at her sister, all thoughts of the picnic gone from her mind now. "Oh boy! Do you realize what this means? This really *is* a haunted, house. Gosh, history just took on a whole new meaning. Wow! Do you think that there's a chance that we might see them too? Just wait until the boys hear about this. Talk about creepy. Come on hurry up and get dressed so that we can tell them." She tried to hurry her sister up.

Between the two of them, Michelle was eventually dressed in her usual jeans and tee shirt. Michelle pulled on her trainers as Katie tried to comb her long hair and tie it back into a ponytail. Everything seemed to take longer than usual because they were hindering each other. Eventually she was ready and they went in search of their brothers.

By the time Michelle had retold her story to the two boys, they were just as excited as their sisters were, secretly though the older children still had their doubts. Katie really wanted to believe but was her sister just dreaming it all up. It was possible. The boys still really believed it was all fantasy but they promised to check the internet and carry out some investigations. They may as well as all their friends were away on holiday and with the phones and internet being installed today it would give them something to do.

If anyone had walked into the kitchen in the early hours of that morning they would have found the room to be icy cold despite the Aga cooker being on. The ghost children were sitting round the table talking. Victoria Michelle had just finished telling the others how her visit with Michelle had gone.
"We know she believes but do you think her brothers and sister will believe her when she tells them in the morning?" Isabelle asked
"I hope so. I really hope so." Victoria Michelle replied crossing her fingers.
"Well, if they don't, we will just have to resort to other methods because one way or another they just *have* to believe. There isn't much time left to be gentle." David said fiercely and determinedly.

Chapter Four

NICHOLAS'S GHOSTLY EXPERIENCE

After breakfast, the four children walked down to the pool. This was their own special place. They could talk about their ghost without their parents hearing them. "Just imagine it; we have our very own haunted house." Michelle said for the umpteenth time.

"Not only one ghost but several of them if what you say is true." Christopher corrected his sister. He was still a little skeptical.

"Of course, it's true. You saw the brooch, didn't you? I couldn't make something like this up, could I? If you all remember correctly, I told you when we first saw the house that there was something weird about it, but oh no you wouldn't believe me, would you? You all knew better, or thought you did and now when I've been proved right you're trying to say I'm telling fibs. Well I'm not so there," a very indignant Michelle cried.

"Okay! Okay! Calm down, I'm sorry. I believe you. There's nae need tae blow a fuse." Christopher quickly tried to placate his sister "You kept inferring that your ghost was still living in the house. You said that she said that she lives here with her brother, nursemaid and guardian. Present tense, as if they were all still alive. That doesn't make any sense. Did she say anything about how they all died? I mean she must have died if she's a ghost.

Did she die in the house? What about the others? These 'visions'" (making speech marks with his fingers) "that she has from her past, did she tell you about them? How many of them are there and has she contacted any of them or are you the only one she has spoken to?" He quizzed his sister.
"No, I'm sorry; I don't know anything else, only what I already told you." Michelle answered regretfully. She was happier now that he was finally taking her seriously.
"Well never mind." Katie replied for her brother. Katie had been quiet for some time and the others looked at her expectantly.

They all knew their sister extremely well. When she was quiet like that it meant, she was working something out, like a plan of action. She was a born organizer. This time proved to be no exception and it was no surprise to anyone when she said. "Now here is what we will do. First, Michelle the very next time you see your ghost friend and you will see her again I'm sure of it. Find out the names and dates and ages of any other ghosts here and how they all died, including your friend Michelle. Once we have all the relevant information, we can either check it out on the internet, maybe on one of those family history sites or if we have no luck on the net we can go to the library and see if we can verify any of it in the history books. Meanwhile we can still check out the history of the house. Dad was left a book on the house's history when he bought the house. It was left on a shelf in dad's study. The estate agent must have left it there or something. I saw it when we were helping him unpack his books. In fact, we can go check it now if you want? Perhaps we'll get more information about the Victorian Michelle from it than we know already. It seems so strange us having the same surname. I wonder if it is a coincidence, or if she is one of our ancestors. I think she must be, what do you guys think?" She asked the others.

"Maybe or maybe not. That would be some coincidence though if she was an ancestor. Come on, let's go look now. What are we waiting for, Christmas?" Christopher taunted, already on his way back to the house.

Unfortunately, the children were interrupted before they could even begin to look for the book. Their parents were waiting for them to go on the promised picnic. As it was such a hot day it had been decided to have the picnic at the seaside.

The children loved going to the beach. Having been brought up in the countryside, the only time they ever went to the beach was during the summer when they went on trips like this one or went down south to stay with their Grandparents who lived near a beach.

Michelle's ghost was soon forgotten in the activities of the day. The family had a great time on the beach, swimming, sunbathing, playing with their beach ball and having their picnic.

It was late when they arrived back home. After the beach, their parents had taken them to the cinema to see the latest Super Hero movie. On the way home from the cinema they had stopped off at the fish and chip shop to have their supper. This was to save their Mother the chore of having to cook supper so late.

Everyone was happy but tired by the time they arrived home. The children went straight to bed. For once there were no arguments or mischief by any of the children. No quarreling with each other about who used the toilet first and who did or did not brush their teeth. They did what had to be done, tumbled into their beds and were asleep almost as soon as their heads hit their pillows.

It was almost two o'clock in the morning when Nicholas heard the noise. He woke up startled. He was puzzled. What had wakened him? The noise had come from outside. It had sounded just like horses' hooves walking on cobbles. He listened and sure enough he could hear more noises. Yes, it was definitely horses' hooves he could hear. He could hear them whinnying now and he could hear hammering noises.

He wondered where the horses had come from. He knew that the old stables were situated just across from the house. There was also the old blacksmith's place just off from the stables but there were no horses. There hadn't been horses on the property in many years. He listened some more not sure if he had imagined the noises or maybe still dreaming. No, the noises were still there, the hammering and the clip clopping of hooves, horses whinnying and now he could also hear voices.

Nicholas was a little afraid but his curiosity got the

better of him. He quietly got out of bed and without switching on his light he felt his way across to the window. There was still a full moon in the sky so he could see quite clearly. When he looked out the window he could not believe his eyes. He blinked, rubbed his eyes, and then looked again. Yes, they were still there. He just couldn't believe what he saw. He even gave himself a hard pinch to his left arm, just to make sure that he really was awake, ouch! It hurt. Yes, he was definitely awake alright. He could still see the scene outside.

It was like watching an historical film on TV. There was a hive of activity below his window. The stables and the blacksmith's forge seemed to be in good repair. The Blacksmith was busy hammering. He was in the middle of shoeing a horse. There were other horses too in the stables. Some were obviously riding horses but there were also some larger horses used for working on the land ploughing the fields probably, he thought.

The blacksmith was in the middle of shoeing one of the shire horses. While he worked, he spoke to a young boy of about nine years of age. The young boy was helping the blacksmith by holding the horse still. They spoke in the old Gaelic language. Nicholas recognized the language as being very like the one that his grandmother had tried to teach him last summer.

He could only understand some of the words from the conversation that took place below his window. He heard the word deamhan, which meant devil and then the name Angus McGregor. Down below in the court yard, Nicholas could clearly hear the conversation between the old blacksmith and the young boy. They weren't very happy. "Gu bheil deamhan!" (That devil) The young boy said. "Tha e a 'choire gu bheil ar daoine leis an acras." (It is his fault that our people are starving.)

"Chan eil! 'S e an gaiseadh a 'bhuntàta a bu choireach airson a 'ghorta." (No! It is the potato blight to blame for the famine.) The old man reasoned.

"ar daoine bheilear a 'sparradh a-mach às na dachaighean aca a dhèanamh do chaoraich." (Our people are being forced out of their homes to make way for sheep) The boy argued angrily. This made the old blacksmith angry. "Aidh! Tha salach sasenach!" (Aye! The dirty sasanach!) "Tha ean-iochdmhor fear ùr again uachdaran." (He is a cruel man our new Laird.)

From the conversation, he had just overheard Nicholas surmised that the discussion had had something to do with people being hungry due to some kind of famine and that it was somehow the fault of "that devil" Angus McGregor. Nicholas could tell that the blacksmith did not like Angus McGregor by the way he had spat on the ground after saying his name.

Just then Nicholas saw a woman appear. She looked to be in her mid-thirties. She was wearing a long gray linen dress, with a tartan shawl around her head and shoulders. She was carrying a bucket and looked quite tired and sad. The blacksmith was wearing an old linen shirt and old worn tartan trousers. The boy was dressed in the same fashion as the old man except he wore a jacket over his shirt. Nicholas looked closer at both the trousers and the woman's shawl. They all wore the same tartan but as it was not the McGregor tartan and as he was unable to recognize which tartan it was, he could not tell which clan they were from.

Suddenly the young boy looked up towards Nicholas's window. He stared straight up at Nicholas for a few seconds and then turned back to the old blacksmith. He spoke quickly to him and was obviously quite agitated. As he spoke, he pointed up to the window where Nicholas was still looking. "a 'coimhead air 'ghille 'ga fhaicinn e aon dhuibh." (Look at the boy, see him, he is one of them.) He stared up at Nicholas with anger and hatred showing in his eyes. The blacksmith turned around to see what the boy was pointing to. He too looked at Nicholas with the same hatred and anger shining in his eyes. He too pointed up at him and as Nicholas moved quickly away from the window, out of their view he could swear the man mouthed the word "a dh 'aithghearr." (Soon.) Before spitting on the ground again.

Nicholas felt frightened and was more than a little shaky. His room suddenly became very cold. It was so cold that he could see his breath. A strange dark mist swirled around the room coming to stop right in front of him. Then right in front of his eyes the mist formed itself into the boy from the court yard. Poor Nicholas was terrified. He was shaking quite violently from the coldness of the room and the fear of what was happening.

Suddenly before the boy could say or do anything, several balls of white light appeared surrounding Nicholas. The ghost boy scowled at the lights then laughed. It was a strange eerie sound. It was a wicked evil laugh. “Soon.” He whispered into Nicholas’s ear before turning once more into a black mist and disappearing. The balls of white light too quickly disappeared.

The room once again grew warmer and started to look more normal again. Nicholas let out a huge shaky sigh of relief. After a few moments of standing as still and as silent as he could, he plucked up the courage to have another peek out of the window. This time all he could see were the old stables in need of repair. No sign remained of the scene that Nicholas had witnessed only moments before.

He stood at the window for a few moments longer before he crept silently back to his bed. He was thirsty and could have done with going downstairs to the kitchen to get a drink of milk. However, after his recent frightening experience, he was feeling quite spooked. Instead of fetching his drink, he curled himself up into his usual fetal position pulling the duvet over his head. He fell asleep thinking about what he had just witnessed and trying to figure out what it all meant.

Once again, the ghosts were round the kitchen

table discussing the events of the night. “That was close. Do you think he would have hurt him?” David asked.

“No. I think he just meant to frighten him. At least now he will believe his sister and hopefully he will persuade the others to believe in our existence too.” Victoria Michelle replied.

“They must believe him. Time will be running out soon.” Isabelle said quietly

Chapter Five

THE BOOK

Nicholas was first down to breakfast the following morning. Now that his mother was pregnant, she needed more help and rest. To help her, and especially since they were on holiday, the children took it in turn to set the breakfast table and prepare breakfast. Once ready, they would then take her breakfast to her in bed.

Being a farmer, Mr. McGregor was always up and working on the farm long before anyone else. Before her pregnancy, Mrs. McGregor too would be up early to collect the eggs from the chickens, prepare breakfast for the children, her husband and the farm hands. The move along with her advanced pregnancy had tired her out and the Doctor had advised her to rest more.

The children had now taken over some of her tasks. There were no chickens on this farm yet as the new hen house was still in the process of being built. It was too late in the season to grow anything on the land here but as Mr. McGregor still owned their previous farm his Farm Manager was now living in the old farm house and would oversee the running of that farm whilst Mr. McGregor organized the new place. He would be close by in case his wife needed him.

Today it was Nicholas's turn to prepare breakfast. He had laid the table, taken the tray into his mum and had almost finished his own cereal, when the others finally joined him at the table.

He listened in silence to his siblings teasing him because for once he was the first one up. Usually he needed to be called on a few times before he would finally get up out of bed. Eventually, they stopped teasing. It was no fun when he wouldn't react and retaliate.

"Okay brother, what gives? Why are you so quiet Nick?" His twin asked, becoming quite concerned at her brother's unusual lack of response.

"Oh, nothing much, I guess I'm still a little tired after what happened during the night." Nick answered quietly, pretending a casualness, which he didn't really feel.

He had intended to get a little revenge on the others, but his excitement was too great and he found himself telling the others everything that had happened in the middle of the night. Well almost everything. He kept quiet about being so scared he had slept with his quilt tightly around him, too terrified to move.

"Weren't you scared?" Michelle questioned him.

"I'll bet you were," taunted Christopher.

"No! Of course I wasn't. Why should I be scared? Michelle wasn't when she saw her ghosts." Nick lied arrogantly.

"But that's different “declared Michelle.

"Why is it different?" Nick asked beginning to lose his temper.

"Cos, it just is. My ghost was friendly but your ghosts are not nice. They sound evil," argued his sister." Just like I tried to tell you all, this house is evil"

"Don't start squabbling you two. Let's think about what we do now." Katie quickly tried to calm the situation.

"Well I thought that we'd have a look at that old history book which I found on the desk. We've now got even more things to look up in it," replied Nicholas, abandoning the quarrel with his younger sister.

Christopher thought that this was a good plan. "Good idea let's fetch it now," he shouted excitedly. He was really getting into the ghost thing now. It was one thing for Michelle to say she saw ghosts; he could put that down to her overactive imagination. However, if his big brother claimed to see ghosts when he was usually as skeptical as he was himself then he believed too.

The four children made their way to their father's study. In fact, it was a spare bedroom that he had converted into his study and office room. Along the whole length and breadth of one wall ran the shelves that housed his books. In front of the window, was the large desk, upon which sat the computer, word processor and printer. It was here that Mr. McGregor dealt with the business side of his farm. Apart from the desk and chair, the only other pieces of furniture in the room were two couches, with a coffee table in between them. They were next to a fireplace. Mr. McGregor had thought that the large window would help to maximise the light and the real fire would look cozy in the winter when he would be using his office more often.

The book, which the children wanted to study, was lying on their father's desk. They took it across to one of the couches and somehow managed to squeeze all four of them onto the one couch. The two girls, who were sat in the middle, held the book open on their knees, and this is how they studied the book.

It was an old book with a brown leather-bound cover. Inside the book cover they found a detailed family tree. The children were fascinated especially as it contained their own names. They were confused. How could this old book be so up to date? Well they already had one question answered. This was indeed a family home and the ghosts, or most of them at least, were family.

The information found in the book was so interesting that soon all four children were totally absorbed by it. They found out that the house had once been owned by a McGregor. In fact, the McGregor family had owned all this land and quite a lot of the area surrounding the farm.

After reading this information the children grew very excited. Here was the proof that the ghosts in the house were long dead ancestors of theirs. When the family had first moved into the house their father had told them he had felt a great sense of well-being. As if the house had welcomed them all. He had felt that he had finally come home. At the time, they had all laughed and said he was being silly, but now, after reading this, perhaps he wasn't as silly as they had all thought.

According to the book, the house had been owned by a number of people for short periods of time only. No one had kept the house beyond a few months at a time, before moving quickly out again. They had all been frightened away by *"fearsome" apparitions.* However, according to the book, these *"fearsome" apparitions* only showed up when non-members of the clan McGregor owned the house.

Michelle was fascinated. "Wow! I wonder what these fearsome apparitions look like. I don't think we've seen them yet."

"Of course not silly!" Christopher scoffed. "We won't see them because we are family."

"Oh, yes. I forgot. Sorry." Michelle apologised. "Do you think that is why the workmen left in such a great hurry? Do you remember? Before we moved in, when we first saw the house, it looked as if people had left in a rush. Everything had just been left?"

"Yes, that is probably why. It makes sense now". Chris answered her. "We won't see them because we are all McGregors. Being *family,* we have nothing to fear from them."

There was silence whilst the others thought about this. Nicholas was the first one to speak. "You forget. The book is wrong. What about what I saw last night? I don't think they were family. These ghosts were fierce and frightening. *They* really didn't like me. They weren't welcoming at all".

Nicholas pointed out. "In fact, they were really scary".
"I wonder why you saw them. Unless, it was because they were trying to tell you something?" Katie asked.
"More like gloat about something." Nick replied. "Something is going to happen and soon. He couldn't wait to tell me."

This made sense to the others. "Okay, we know that these ghosts you saw last night can't be family ghosts so perhaps Michelle was right when she said that maybe you saw them for a reason and what about the lights you saw? How many did you say there were?" Chris queried.
"I saw five. They were all around me." Nick replied
"Do you think that they could have been the good ghosts trying to keep you safe?" Interrupted Kate.
"Mmm. That sounds about right. The ghost boy certainly didn't like it when they suddenly appeared and he vanished very quickly afterwards." Nick answered.
"Hmm! Maybe the book will give us a clue about what that was all about" Chris suggested.

The children continued with their reading. The book began to mention a curse, which had been placed on the house in the year 1812. This was a few years after the McGregor family had bought the land from the Clan Chief of the Campbells. He had sold the land in order to "clear" it to make room for his sheep. It was during this clearance that the Laird had forced the tenant Campbells out of their homes and off their land.

Their house had once belonged to the Clan Chief. It was said that the new landlord was responsible for the deaths of two of his tenants when he had ordered their croft to be burnt. "Michelle, do you know what we mean when we talk about the Highland clearances?" Nicholas asked, fully expecting to have to explain all about it.

"Of course I do. I have read all about it in school. My project for last term included reading a book called 'The Desperate Journey' by Kathleen Fiddler. It was very good. Do you know that some people were even burned out of their homes and were forced to live elsewhere and some even moved to countries such as America, Canada and Australia? That is why there are people all over the world visit Scotland claiming to have Scottish blood." She finished.

"History was my best subject last year." Chris interrupted. "I really enjoyed learning about the clearances and about the Jacobites and Culloden. I would have liked to have been a Jacobite." He went on to explain what he knew about the Highland Clearances.

When the Jacobites lost at Culloden in 1746, the Government did not want any recurrence so they set out to destroy Highland life. People were no longer allowed to speak Gaelic. The number of Lairds who spoke Gaelic dropped and Landowners who spoke English increased. These land owners preferred to live in the south as there, was more going on. To be able to afford their rich lifestyles in the South they needed money.

Highland Estates moved from farming, which needed many tenants, to sheep farming which was more profitable but needed more land. To make way for the sheep people were removed from the land to the coast to begin new occupations such as fishing and working in the kelp industry. He explained to a puzzled Michelle that kelp was a type of seaweed which once grown in deep water and harvested had various uses.

Some landowners forced their tenants from the land to the coast so that the land was free for sheep and their tenants would bring in even more money from working as fishermen and kelp workers as kelp was profitable too. During this time, most workers were too poor to emigrate and landowners would not allow them to emigrate as they were needed to work. Later, once the kelp came down in value the highlanders were forced to either immigrate to other countries or move down south to work in factories.

Christopher went on to tell his brother and sister about a man called Patrick Seller who was a sheep farmer who had been hired by the Stafford family to work with the sheep on their Sutherland Estates. Part of his duties had been to supervise the eviction and forced move of his tenants from his estates to Brora on the coast. He would pull down the roofs of their houses and set fire to the roof trees to stop anyone trying to rebuild the house. Some elderly people who had been evicted were murdered and he had been tried for this but had been allowed to go free,

The Crofters Act in 1886 ended the clearances although there were no more crofters to evict.

"All those poor people, forced out of their homes to live in totally alien environments, first on the coast and then again into the cities. The hardships they must have endured, having to leave their families, their friends, the homes they loved, to go and live in strange new places, living in cramped towns or risk dying in overcrowded and disease infested ships, starving and frightened at the thought of having to start again in strange new lands." Michelle felt sad.

Katie put her arm round her sister and gave her a quick cuddle. "That is why there are people from all over the world now who visit Scotland claiming to have Scottish Ancestry". Katie explained.

"Yes, and it was all because of greedy land owners wanting more money to fund their rich lifestyles." Nick angrily continued. "Just think our ancestor could have been one of them. I don't like him. Maybe he deserved to be cursed."

Christopher was puzzled. "Maybe, but what I would like to know", he frowned. "Is why, if the curse is supposed to be lifted once a McGregor owns and inhabits the house again, then why have Nick and Michelle seen the ghosts?"

"Good question. Apart from Nick, I don't think we have seen the bad ghosts. I think what Nick saw was a warning of some kind. Maybe the ghosts which we have seen are different and have nothing to do with the curse." Katie explained patiently. "I can't find any mention in the book of the ghosts which were seen by Nick and Michelle. Perhaps

they have only appeared now at this time because we are family."
"Yes, you could be right ", Nick agreed with his twin.
"Of course, I am right. I am always right, am I not?" teased Katie.

Nick took the bait. "Okay, okay, big head. You won't get out through that door if your head grows much bigger", he teased her back.

Christopher was still puzzled. "Wait a minute! There is something else which I don't understand". He interrupted impatiently. He was used to the constant teasing which went on between his brother and sister and normally both him and his little sister enjoyed listening to them but this time his mind was on other matters. Katie sighed, "Okay then, what else do you not understand".
"Well then Smarty pants, solve this one if you can. If the curse was lifted once a McGregor owned the place again and if the Victorian Michelle was also a McGregor, why was the curse not lifted then?" Christopher finished in a rush.
"That is another good question. Maybe we will find the answer further on in the book. Let's have a look and see". Katie replied.

Unfortunately, before the children could investigate further, they heard their mother calling them. It was lunchtime. The children groaned. Now they would not get a chance to finish the book for a whole week. Their Mother was taking them to visit their Grandparents after lunch. As her parents lived in Fife, Mrs. McGregor did not get the chance to visit very often. When they did manage, the visit usually lasted at least a week.

Mrs. McGregor was looking forward to her visit. Her plans included shopping for baby clothes as well as buying new clothes for her children to go back to school with. She had planned with her own Mother exactly what and where they would do their shopping. She missed her parents and was eagerly looking forward to her visit.

The children tidied up their mess of crisp packets and iron bru tins from the coffee table. Nicholas carefully put the book away where they would easily find it again then went to join their mum in the kitchen for lunch.

That night the ghost children sat around the kitchen table discussing the events of the day. They were happy and excited that the children now seemed to be believing in them but frustrated and impatient at the delay whilst the children went on holiday.

Time was important and if the children were to be saved there was very little time left.

"How long are they away for? It might be too late by the time they get back" One little ghost boy asked. He was quite annoyed that things were not moving quickly enough.

"I pray not. For all our sakes, I hope not" Victoria replied sadly.

Chapter Six

VICKI'S WARNING

One week later, the children were back home. They had thoroughly enjoyed their visit to their grandparents. Their visit had coincided with the visit of their Uncle Bill and Auntie Laura and their three cousins. That this had all been carefully and deliberately planned had never even occurred to the four children.

Their week had consisted of picnics, swimming, shopping and cycling. A couple of days had been spent in Edinburgh where they had travelled on the trams, visited Edinburgh castle, and climbed Arthur's seat where they had enjoyed a warm but windy picnic. The Science Museum had been next on their list with a visit to the Museum of Childhood. The children had found their visit to the Camera Obscura particularly enjoyable and fascinating. They had all said it was great fun but sore on their feet.

In fact, they had had such a great time they had almost forgotten about the existence of their resident ghosts. Almost, but not quite. It had been hard to forget, especially once they were back home. It had been a few days since their return and so far, no one had made any move towards the study or the book. The children were still full of excitement and energy from their holiday. The house was growing restless and impatient. Trouble was brewing.

The children had only gone back to their book reading after a series of events which had culminated in not one but two near accidents and their mother screaming and telling their father that she had seen ghosts. At first when items in the house began to go missing then reappear in a separate part of the house, Mrs. McGregor thought she was being forgetful and put the blame on her pregnancy. Milk from the fridge would appear in the oven. Clean clothes would appear in the dirty laundry basket.

Even more unsettling was when ornaments from the living room would be found in the bathroom or the kitchen. The doorbell would ring for no reason or the TV would switch itself on with the sound up so loud it would wake everyone up in the middle of the night. Pictures hung securely on the wall would suddenly fall down for no apparent reason.

The first near accident was when Mrs. McGregor almost slipped on a broken egg which was on the floor just inside the kitchen door. However just as Mrs. McGregor had been about to walk into the kitchen the door blew shut in her face preventing her from walking in and slipping on the egg. She could not open the door and had eventually called for her husband to help get the door open. To her astonishment, the door opened very easily and he immediately saw the egg broken on the floor and cleaned it up before any damage could be done.

The second near miss had it succeeded would have been fatal and ended up in the death of Mrs. McGregor. She was on the landing at the top of stairs and due to her being heavily pregnant with twins did not see the shoe lying on the top stair. Just as she was about to step down onto the stair, she felt her arms being grabbed and she was pulled backwards by an unseen force. She was helpless to do anything but go backwards as she was propelled to do so. She screamed. As she felt her arms being released she could feel a rush of air as two balls of light floated quickly past her on both sides. The balls of light stopped and hovered over the top stair shining on the shoe before quickly floating down the stairs and vanishing. Hearing his wife screaming Mr. McGregor came running up the stairs to see what was wrong.

At first when he saw the shoe on the stair he thought his wife had injured herself and the babies. After making sure his wife was okay and settled in her room resting after her fright, the children were summoned and severely lectured to about the dangers of leaving shoes, toys and other items lying around the floor. Michelle tried to tell her father that all her clothes, shoes and toys had been tidied away in her room before she left her room that morning.

Mr. McGregor had been too angry to listen. It had taken him some time to calm his poor wife down after her fright. She was resting now but was now convinced that the house was haunted and was trying to get rid of her and the babies. She was lucky she said that her guardian angels were looking after her.

Mr. McGregor was very worried about his wife.

This pregnancy was not going well. There was nothing wrong with the babies but his wife's mental state was becoming fragile. He had thought her little break might have helped relax her but since she got back she wasn't sleeping, claiming to keep hearing crying coming from the nursery. She was wakening up about the same time every night hearing noises and muffled crying. She would see flickering lights in the hallway. He had gotten in an electrician to check the lights and wiring but everything was working normally with no problems highlighted. He was at a loss to understand.

She had told him she was having weird dreams and kept thinking that she was being watched. It had given him goosebumps just listening to all his wife had told him. He had tried to persuade her to see a Doctor but she had calmed down and persuaded him that it was just her hormones causing all her problems.

Secretly though Mrs. McGregor really did think there was a problem and it had nothing to do with her hormones. No, it was time she consulted with the family witch. Her Aunt Winnie was a Wicca and spiritualist. She was also a very gifted psychic. She would give her a call and invite her for a visit. With this thought in mind she went to have a rest quite calmly knowing she could rely on her Aunt to sort everything out.

As their father was talking the children were horrified to see writing appear on the mirror behind him "Ha! Ha! Soon!" Seeing his children's expressions, he turned around to see what they were staring at and why their attention was not focused on him. The writing had disappeared. Seeing nothing he turned to face the children again angrier than ever with them. His punishment for them was grounding. They were to remain in the house for two whole days. They were to make sure their rooms were spotless and nothing was out of place.

The children were angry. Not at their father grounding them but at the fact that someone was trying to harm their mother and the unborn babies. Could it be the little ghost girl Michelle had encountered? It did not seem likely but she had told Michelle about other ghosts living in the house. It was time to find out more and put a stop to the haunting. Michelle felt quietly smug. She had tried to warn everyone the house was evil but they hadn't listened and now she had been proved correct.

Now they were once again back in the study having a look at the book. They had wanted to find out more about what was going on in the house and about the Victorian Michelle, but what Katie had just read out to them had left them more than a little mystified. They had read that Michelle had indeed been a McGregor. However according to the book, she had not as they had assumed died young, nor had she died in the house. She had grown up, married and had lived till she was quite an old woman. She was in fact a direct ancestor of theirs She was their great, great, great, great Grandmother. She had been seventy-four years

old when she had died in Edinburgh, so why did Michelle see her when she was a little girl? The children were puzzled. How could that be? Surely her ghost should be that of an old woman?
"Maybe the book will tell us why" Nick suggested. "Katie read some more."

Katie read aloud again and they found out that she was born in the year 1837, which was the same year that Queen Victoria came to the throne. She was christened Michelle Victoria McGregor. The Michelle part of her name came from her French born mother whose Christian name was Michelle-Marie. Her middle name was after Queen Victoria. Her surname of course was from her Father who was Scottish. Her Father's family had stayed in Edinburgh most of the time when he was a boy. In fact, her Father had been the last McGregor to have been born in the house on McGregor land.

Just after his birth the land had been sold. "He must have known about the curse and that is why he sold the house. He never could have thought that someone further down the family line would buy it back. It must have been our great, great, great, great, great, great Grandfather's tenants who cursed the house then," Christopher told the others cleverly.
"That would make him Vicki's Grandfather", Michelle informed them, proving that she could count too.
"Vicki? Vicki who?" asked a puzzled Nicholas. "Oh yes. I know who you mean. Vicki as in Michelle

Victoria."
"Yes. It's much less confusing, don't you think?" confirmed Michelle. "I hope she won't mind us calling her that. Somehow, I can't quite think of her as my great, great, great, great Grandmother. I remember now who it is she reminded me of. It's me. She looks like me. Its mind boggling, don't you think?"

The others nodded their heads agreeing with their sister. It was hard to imagine the young girl their sister had just described.

"Just think Michelle, you must be named after our, now let me get this correct, our great, great, great, great Grandmother. Mum did say that Michelle - Marie was an old family name. I always wondered where the name came from and now I know." Katie excitedly informed her sister.

"Katie! You are missing the point. Think about it. What have we just read?" Nicholas interrupted his twin impatiently.

"Oh, yes.... I see what you mean." Katie said slowly after a moment's silence. "Gosh! How strange. It doesn't make any sense, does it?"

The four children were very quiet for a while. They were very puzzled. They were each still trying to work out just how it could be that Michelle had seen the ghost of their great, great, great, great Grandmother as a young girl and not as an old lady. "Are you absolutely certain that you really did see her? You didn't just dream about her, did you?" Christopher finally asked.

Michelle was more than a little annoyed at having

her story put in doubt now. “You know I saw her. Of course, I did not dream her up. You saw the brooch, didn’t you? Any way how could I know so much about her if I had only just dreamt about her? The book confirms what I told you about her and I ‘ve certainly never read this book before.”

Katie tried to soothe her sister’s hurt feelings. “Okay Michelle, we know that you didn’t lie. There must be some reason as to why Vicki has appeared to you as a child and not as an old lady, but why appear at this particular stage in her life? What is so significant about this point in her life? She has to be trying to tell us something don’t you think?” She asked the others.

Before the others could say anything, Christopher excitedly explained the theory, which had just come to him. “You said that her parents had recently disappeared in mysterious circumstances and that she is very unhappy. Maybe that is why she has come back at this particular time in her life. Maybe she wants us to find out what happened to them.”

Katie gave him a quick hug. “Christopher, you are a genius! Of course, you are absolutely right. That *is* why she has appeared to Michelle as a child.” She turned to her younger sister. “Michelle, you must try to get in contact with Vicki tonight. Find out all you can about her ‘visions’. Maybe she can tell us something more about the ghosts Nick saw”.

“I can do a search on the internet to see if anything is known about the house.” Chris suggested. Just then they were interrupted by the sound of their mother shouting for them to come and wash up for supper.

Shortly after supper the children went to bed. As Michelle prepared for bed, she was busy wondering just how she was supposed to manage to contact Vicki. On both their previous encounters, the ghost had just appeared without any conjuring up from her. Michelle need not have worried though because just as she had settled herself into bed, Vicki appeared.

Just like Michelle, Vicki was dressed for bed. Her cotton nightdress covered her from neck to toe and was of a typical Victorian style. Michelle looked down at her own pink pajamas. The two styles had not one thing in common. The two girls stared at each other for a few seconds and then both started to laugh. When their laughter stopped, Michelle said, “I was just thinking about you. I wanted to see you.” Vicki’s answer surprised her. “I know. That is why I have come. “

“You know? How? I mean, how could you know that I was thinking about you?” Michelle asked bewilderedly.

“I do not know how exactly. I only know that you needed to see me. I know that it is very important that we help one another. I have been watching you with your family. You have a very nice family. You are all very happy together. I am sorry for what your poor Mother has been put through. Please believe me when I tell you she did not suffer from my actions. They were nothing to do with me. I tried to prevent them.” Vicki quickly assured

Michelle.

"It was you who stopped my Mum falling down the stairs wasn't it?" Michelle asked.

"Yes" Confirmed Vicki "But I had help. We did not mean to cause your Mother fright but we had to prevent her fall and show her the shoe."

"Who put the shoe on the stair if it wasn't you? How did you know it was there?" Michelle was puzzled.

"The others put it there to cause mischief. I did tell you that we are not alone here. Most are friendly but there are a few who enjoy making mischief and some who are just evil" Vicki tried to explain.

She took a deep sigh before adding very seriously, "There is much worse to come and we must work together if we are to prevent what is to come" This house however is evil and please do not ask me how I know this. I just sense this. This house is bad for you all. There is danger and much unhappiness coming soon for you all if you remain here." Vicki explained. "You too know this. When you first came here, you felt the bad vibrations too."

"Yes, I did feel the bad vibrations too and I did try to tell the others, but I don't understand how you know how I felt then?" Michelle insisted even more bewildered now.

"How I know is not important. Please just accept that I do know. Now let us please change the subject." Vicki pleaded worriedly.

She could see that Michelle was becoming frightened and upset. Her calming voice had an immediate effect on the young Michelle. She could tell that her friend was worried. "Okay. I'm sorry. I was just curious." Michelle consoled her friend. "Why don't you tell me something about yourself and your family?"

Vicki smiled. "Very well then. What was that word you used? Okay? Okay then. I was born in Edinburgh in 1837 which was the same year as Princess Victoria became Queen. For this reason, my parents named me Michelle Victoria. My first name is Michelle, after my Mother and my middle name is Victoria, after her Majesty. As you already guessed I have a small brother and now at the age of ten years I am an orphan." She said sadly as a tear trickled slowly out of one eye.

Michelle tried to comfort the little ghost girl. "I know and I am really sorry. Let's not talk about that just yet. Why don't you tell me what life is like for you under the reign of Queen Victoria? Do you go to school?" Michelle asked.

"School? Oh, no. A governess teaches me at home. My Papa was thinking about sending me to a private school for young ladies once we returned to Edinburgh. My Uncle, however, is undecided on this matter and may decide to continue my education with a governess. He is a very strict disciplinarian and I admit that I am more than slightly afraid of him." Vicki confided.

"Do you mean that he believes in 'breaking the rod to spare the child'? I read somewhere that this was very common in 'Victorian times'. I know it's a saying but not too sure what it really means though" She smiled before having another not so pleasant thought. "Oh, dear he doesn't beat you, does he?"

Michelle asked, feeling quite shocked at the thought of this very pretty and fragile looking girl being beaten with a stick.
"Oh! No! No!" Vicki was quick to reassure her. "My Uncle Jamie is very strict but I do not believe that he would hit me." She tried to explain. "You see, Uncle Jamie has never married and so has not had much dealing with children. He tries his best and I am sure that he means to be kind, but he is not Papa. I am mostly left to the care of my governess. I have no doubt that when little William is older my Uncle will have more to do with him. I am just a girl and so therefore not very intelligent. He will make sure that I am taught all that will be necessary to run a household and find a good husband for me when the time is right. After all, a woman's place is in the home is it not?" She asked Michelle.

Michelle almost laughed out loud. She didn't know whether to feel angry or sad at how her new friend had been brought up. "Not any more it isn't. We are living in the twenty-first century now. Nowadays some women work whilst their men stay at home to look after the children. Women can be anything they want to be. All children go to school five days a week, forty weeks a year. Girls learn the same subjects as boys do and attend the same schools and classes. There are women Lawyers, women Doctors and there has even been two women Prime Ministers for the UK. Here in Scotland our First Minister is a woman too. In fact, women, can do any job a man can do and vice versa providing they have the right qualifications."

Michelle finished talking as she noticed the astonished look on Vicki's face.
"Is that really true? Oh, my Goodness! I wish that I had been born in your time." She said wistfully. "In my time, we are brought up to believe that a woman's place is in the home. Not everyone goes to school. Four years ago, in 1843 there was an act passed in Parliament. This act was called the Factory Act. It stated that all children must attend school for part of their day. Those children who work in factories spend their morning in school and their afternoons at work. Only last year in 1846, here in Scotland, in Glasgow a public school was opened. It was called The Glasgow Academy. It is one of only a few public schools in Scotland. Unfortunately for us girls, we are taught only the things that will help us to run a household when we marry. We are taught subjects such as drawing, needlework, painting and household management. We are also taught a little of the cultural subjects such as French and literature. My Governess, who is a blue stocking says that girls are just as intelligent as boys, but my Uncle says that is not the case and considers it unladylike to have too much learning." Vicki concluded.

Michelle was puzzled. "What is a blue stocking Vicki?" she asked
"A blue stocking is a woman who is interested in learning. My Governess is a blue stocking and knows many things. I am very lucky to have her teach me. Would you like to see the sampler which I am currently working on?" Vicki asked Michelle

politely.
"A sampler? What is a sampler?" Michelle asked, puzzled again. Vicki disappeared for a few minutes. When she returned she was holding a piece of needlework. She held it up to show Michelle. "I brought you this completed piece. I practice my stitches on this. When I leave, I will leave it for you on the floor. You can show your brothers and sister it."

Michelle felt honoured at being given this gift. "Thank you. I would love to have it. I'm afraid that I am not nearly as good as you are at needlework." She said as she admired the neat stitches.

Vicki was pleased at this compliment. "I must go soon. My Governess will be in to check on me very soon," she warned her friend. "We must talk about more unpleasant things now. We must talk about my parents' disappearance. When we first came here, we were very happy. It gave my Papa much pleasure to buy back the house and once again be back in the home of his birth. He was unaware of the curse as my Grandfather had never mentioned the reason for the sale. We were here only for six months when tragedy struck. My parents, for no reason that we can think of just disappeared one night and never came back. We found the door open in the morning, but of my parents, not a trace of them has been found in the months since. It is now approaching a whole year since that fateful night."

Vicki stopped talking and listened for a few seconds, before saying quickly," My Governess is approaching. I can hear her coming. I will leave you the sampler, and remember, when you need me just think about me and I will come to you. Good - Bye for the present." Vicki placed her hand on Michelle's arm, which to Michelle's surprise she could feel. It felt warm, not cold or clammy. "Please pay careful attention to what I have just said" she warned Michelle.

Then she was gone. There was an indentation on the bed where she had been sitting. The sampler just as Vicki had promised was left lying on the floor. Michelle picked it up and after examining it closely for a few moments, placed it carefully under her pillow. She then switched her overhead light off and went to sleep thinking about her latest encounter with Vicki and wondering just which part of their conversation she had to pay careful attention to.

Vicky left Michelle feeling more optimistic having enjoyed talking with her new little friend. She had been quite surprised and pleased at how well Michelle had accepted her and the other ghost's presence in the house. She felt she had played her part well in telling Michelle as much as she was able to about the curse without telling her the full story. Vicky was not alone at feeling frustrated at not being able to give a full explanation about the ghosts in the house. Her friends felt the same frustration but due to the curse itself they were unable to. The children had to figure it out by themselves. However, the resourceful ghost children had gotten round this hurdle by each picking a child and telling their own story. It was in their favour that there were four children this time. By working together, they could finally solve the mystery and lift the curse. Vicky laughed and then sighed. Would there be enough time left to do so though? She went to find the others.

Chapter Seven

MORE GHOSTLY GOINGS ON

Michelle was not the only one to have a ghostly visitation that night. Meanwhile, across the landing in Katie's bedroom, she too was having a visitation. Her ghostly visitor was a young girl about fourteen years of age. From the way in which she was dressed and by her hairstyle, Katie guessed that the girl was probably from the 1940s. Perhaps from the war era? Katie did not find her presence the least bit frightening or threatening. In fact, she thought that the ghost girl looked rather lost and very unhappy. Katie felt sorry for her.

Katie had been lying awake reading, when she had heard a slight tap at her door. Thinking that her sister or one of her brothers probably made it, she had shouted for them to come in. When there had been no reply, and after a second knock, she had got out of her bed and gone to open the door, only to find no one there. She frowned, then shrugging her shoulders closed the door thinking that she must have imagined the tapping noise. She turned away from her door towards her bed intending to get back in.

The ghost girl stood by the bed. She beckoned for Katie to come closer and gave her a smile of encouragement as she said," Please come and sit-down Katie. I will not hurt you. I only wish to talk with you. You have a very pretty name. My name is Isabelle. Isabelle McGregor. I am fourteen years old and I very much need your help please." As she was speaking she wandered restlessly around the room, but finally came to stand directly in front of Katie, who was now sitting on top of her bed.

Katie was a little startled to hear Isabelle call her by her name, but she was a kind girl and could not resist the girl's plea for help. She smiled back at Isabelle and said," Hello Isabelle. I'm not sure how you know my name but I'm very pleased to meet you. Please tell me about yourself and how I can help?" Isabelle's smile grew wider. She was clearly relieved that this first meeting was going so well.

Katie thought that Isabelle was a very pretty girl when she smiled. Isabelle was slightly taller than herself, she guessed, maybe one metre, sixty-one centimeters to her own one metre and fifty-six centimeters. She was slim with dark hair. The dress she was wearing was a style from the Second World War era. She knew this because she had recently studied it in school. She was wearing a short-sleeved light blue flower-patterned dress. It had a round neck and the short sleeves were puffed at the shoulder. It came to below her knee and she wore white ankle socks and brown sandals.

Katie's mum had told her that some war era fashions had briefly made comebacks in 1995, when the country had celebrated fifty years of the ending of the Second World War by having V.E. Commemoration celebrations. Isabelle's rolled hairstyle too had briefly been in fashion during the V.E. Commemorations. Katie could remember seeing photos of her Grandma and Great Auntie dressed up for the celebrations wearing their hair in very similar styles to the style Isabelle had.

After making sure that Katie was sitting comfortably, Isabelle began her story. She had been the only daughter in a family of three boys, all older than herself. They were brought up in the town of Kirkcaldy in Fife. On hearing this Katie just could not help but exclaim. "Kirkcaldy! That is where my parents' families come from too."

"Yes, I know that." Isabelle replied with a laugh. "Your Great great, Grandfather is my cousin. Did you not realize my dear that I can communicate with you, only because we are related? For some reason or other, which I cannot fathom out, I can only show myself to family and only to child members of our clan. Look let me show you how we are connected."

She held out her hand and clicked her fingers. As if by magic a book appeared in her hand. It was the family history book. However, when she went to the page showing the family tree it was incomplete. "Oh Bother! "She exclaimed angrily. She was more than a little frustrated. "I forgot about the curse. Sorry it looks like you must figure out all the connections yourselves. I was hoping we could quicken the process up a little but it seems like there will be no cutting corners and taking short cuts." She sighed. "Let us get comfortable and I shall begin again." She threw the book up in the air and it disappeared.

Isabelle sat down on the bed next to Katie. Katie was a little surprised. She had expected to feel very cold with a ghost next to her but she wasn't. The room was warm and she would swear that she could smell roses in the air.

"We can only show ourselves to family. We are all the same," Isabelle frowned, then as her voice suddenly became serious said, "We were all given the warnings by the ones who had gone before, but we were useless to prevent fate. This time there are four of you and not just one. Together, perhaps you can turn fate to your advantage. I really hope that you can. It would be dreadful if you were all destined to share our fate."

On hearing Katie's horrified gasp, Isabelle stopped what she was about to say and said instead, "I am sorry my dear. I don't mean to alarm you, especially as you probably do not know what I am talking about yet. I think that perhaps I should begin at the beginning, don't you?"

After obtaining Katie's agreement, Isabelle continued with her story. Her brothers, Brian, John and James were all older than she was and all three were in the forces. John and James were both in the Air force and Brian was in the army. All her brothers had been overseas when Isabelle's parents had decided to move out of the town into the country. It would be safer, they had thought.

Isabelle's Father had been badly burned at the beginning of the war. He had been in the Navy when his ship had been bombed. He had been awarded a medal for his bravery in helping his fellow officers and men to escape from their burning ship. During his rescue attempts, he had inhaled a lot of smoke into his lungs, which had damaged them beyond repair. The country air would be much healthier for her Father and safer for them all.

They had moved to this house and for several months had been very happy. Her fathers' health improved to such an extent that he had even started to grow some of his own vegetables. During the war people had been encouraged to grow their own vegetables. Isabelle explained that during the war a lot of foodstuffs had been scarce and many things were rationed. Among those things rationed were - butcher meat, sugar, butter, jam, bacon, eggs and even tinned meat. They had even tried to ration bread, she explained disgustedly but it had not worked out, although it had not been as white as it once was. Fruit such as oranges and bananas were unknown to most children. Her Father had kept some chickens so that they would have a supply of fresh eggs instead of having to use the dried egg substitutes.

Isabelle paused in her story telling to smile reminiscently. "I remember that we had to carry our gas masks with us at all times and our identity cards. At school, we had air raid drills. Being in the country, our school never had an air raid shelter, so when there was an actual air raid, those of us who lived near the school were sent quickly home.

Those children who were left were sent home with us. When the sirens sounded. We stopped everything and ran home. It was frightening at first, but after a while we became very blasé about it all. When the all clear signal sounded, we had to return to school." She laughed at some memory she had recalled. She had a nice laugh, Katie thought. It did not sound in the least bit eerie or ghostly.

Isabelle continued with her story. "As we lived in the country, we did not see much action. The bomber's targets were for the larger towns and cities, so here in the country we did not see the devastation that those bombs caused." She frowned. "No, it was later that I witnessed all that devastation. Everything changed after my parents' disappearance. I did not know then that from that day onwards my fate was sealed for all time." Isabelle continued sadly.

Katie was startled. "Your parents disappeared? What happened to them?" She questioned. Isabelle ignored the interruption. "Did you know that when I lived here, I too saw the ghost of our Victorian ancestor? Unfortunately, I was not as brave as you all are. I was too much of a coward to listen and take notice of her warnings. Please", she said urgently. "Do not make the same mistake that I made. I will now tell you what happened to my parents.

During an air raid one night, I was sleeping upstairs. I slept through it all and next morning when I awoke, I could find no trace of them. Not one single trace. The front door was open but sometime during the night in the middle of an air raid my parents vanished without leaving any clues and were never seen again."

"Oh, you poor thing!" exclaimed Katie sympathetically. "What happened to them? Were they bombed?"
"No. There were no bombs dropped in our neighborhood that night. The bombers had been passing over on their way to try to bomb the Forth Bridge. It was another failed mission by the Germans. No one was ever able to find out what happened to them." Isabelle explained sadly. She covered her eyes and sobbed softly.
"What happened to you afterwards? Did you stay here?" Katie asked, curious.

Isabelle stopped sobbing and sighed deeply, before saying that afterwards she had been sent to stay with relatives of her Mother, her Aunt and Uncle in Clydebank. Her uncle worked in a large aircraft factory making engines for aircraft and her Aunt worked in an ammunition factory making bombs and bullets. A few months later, on the nights of the 13th and 14th March 1941 there were particularly nasty bombing raids. This became known as the Clydebank Blitz. About 400 German planes dropped bombs on Clydebank. Over the two days and nights over a thousand bombs were dropped by the German bombers causing over five hundred deaths and more than six hundred people injured. About four thousand homes were destroyed.

Their home had been destroyed and she had lost her life. "My spirit returned here, to remain here for all eternity with the others, or until such time as the mystery of my parent's disappearance is solved.

Only then will we all be allowed to rest in peace." She finished.

Katie was puzzled. "What do you mean? Others?" She asked as a sudden cold chill ran up her spine. After a short silence, Isabelle spoke. "There are five of us now, but if you do not take notice of these warnings and solve the mystery there will be four more." She warned. "I must go now. Please take care. Solve the mystery Katie, before the same fate happens to you and your brothers and sister." With those words of warning still echoing around the room, Isabelle was gone. The rose smell disappeared with her and all that was left to show that Katie had really had her visit was the indentation on the bed where Isabelle had sat.

Katie felt frightened and confused. What did Isabelle mean? Were they all destined to join the same fate and haunt the house too? She was too tired and frightened to think it all through tonight. She did not want to be on her own, so very quietly, she tiptoed out of her bedroom and across the landing to her sister's room. Michelle was sound asleep so Katie crept quietly into bed with her and eventually managed to fall asleep too.

Isabelle met up with Vicky. They were both happy with the way their meetings had gone. "I thought the meeting with Katie went better than I expected. It was as you thought. She felt sorry for me and her compassion overcame her fear." Isabelle sighed. "I was sorry though for alarming and frightening her at the end but I suppose needs must."

"Yes. It is a shame but now you have gained her trust and her curiosity has been aroused. Tomorrow she will be eager to learn more. Once the boys tell their stories they can begin to put the pieces together. Now let us go find the others to see how their visits were received." The girls made their way to the kitchen to meet the others.

Chapter Eight

FAMILY GHOSTS

Next morning, Michelle was surprised to find her sister in bed beside her. It was not so unusual for the girls to share a bed, but it was usually Michelle crawling in beside Katie for comfort, not the other way around. Michelle was prone to nightmares, particularly after watching horror films, which her parents had now forbidden her to watch.

As today was Michelle's turn to prepare breakfast, she considerately left her sister to sleep. Very quietly, she rose from her bed, dressed and then quietly left the room to go downstairs to begin her chores.

It was about 9.30 a.m. before Katie finally woke up. Her first thoughts were the events of the night before. She had to talk with her brothers and sister as soon as possible. Maybe *they* could figure out what it all meant. She dressed quickly and then went to find them.

Eventually she tracked them down in the study. She arrived there eager to tell her story, only to discover that she was not the only person with a story to tell. Apparently last night had been a night of ghostly visits for them all.

A boy called David had visited Nicholas. He was about twelve years old. He had lived in the house during the early sixties. His parents too had just mysteriously disappeared one night for no apparent reason. He had been killed a few years later in a motor bike accident. However, he had returned to the house as a twelve-year-old ghost. The same age he had been when his parents disappeared.

Christopher too had a similar story to tell. In his case six-year-old twins, Douglas and Calum had visited him. They had lived in the house sometime during the early 1930s. In their case, their parents had also disappeared but their Father had disappeared a year after their Mother. He had been away on business when their Mother had gone missing.

The following year, exactly one-year later he too disappeared from the house in exactly the same circumstances as all the others. Sadly, only two years later Douglas had died from the disease Diphtheria. "Calum met his end in a plane crash in 1959". Christopher explained. "The funny thing is, after they both died their spirits became aged six again, which is the age they were when their Mother first disappeared."

"Curiouser and curiouser", muttered Katie, before beginning the story of her ghostly encounter. There was silence for a few moments after she had finished. Each child coming to terms with all this new knowledge.

"I don't like it. I told you this house had bad vibrations, that there was evil here." Michelle burst out.

"Look, just calm down Michelle. Calm down!" Nicholas soothed his young sister. "Why don't we try to fit all the pieces together and then see what it all means? We can use Dad's white board on the wall as it is blank at the moment. We can play detectives and write down all the clues on the board and see what we have. Maybe we will come up with some answers. Michelle why don't you go find Dad and ask him if we can use his whiteboard? Tell him we will clean it afterwards." Michelle quite liked the idea of playing detective, and as the distraction it was meant to be, it was very successful.

Michelle quickly went to do as she had been asked and as soon as she left the room Katie praised her brother for his quick thinking.

"Do you think that it's wise to let her continue with this? She is starting to get very panicky and spooked and it's not over yet. You never know what might happen next." Christopher asked his older brother and sister.

"I don't think we have any choice in the matter. Whether we like it or not, she is as much a part of this as we all are." Nicholas explained to his younger brother.

"She's tough she'll cope. I know she is very sensitive but remember Aunt Winnie has always insisted that Michelle has inherited her psychic abilities. If she is correct then we may need her psychic gifts. We will just have to keep our eye on her and hope that she copes okay." He added just as Michelle re-entered the room.

"Dad says we can use the board as he has no plans to use it yet for a while. He said the pens for it are in the top drawer in his desk and to remember only to use those pens which are specifically for the whiteboard and not to use normal pens. He said to make sure I told you this as there will be trouble with a capital T if anyone uses normal pens on it." Michelle mimicked her Dad, which had everyone laughing.

Michelle said thoughtfully." You know, I was thinking. We could always get help from Aunt Winnie."

Katie looked quickly at her brothers. And mouthed, "See I told you she was psychic."

Michelle didn't see the look and continued." In fact, I'll bet she is just waiting for us to phone her."

"What makes you think that?" Chris asked curiously.

"Well don't you remember when we saw her at Aunt Laura's, we were telling them about the house and she looked at us strangely and said to remember that she was only a phone call away."

"Oh yes. I remember now." Katie said. "But, I also remember her telling Mum that she was leaving the same day as us to attend the midsummer festival at Stonehenge then off to teach one of her psychic courses in Greece for a month."

"Ah well then, if there's no help from Aunt Winnie, we are on our own." Chris muttered gloomily.

Nicholas found the pen. "Right then let us begin. Fact number one is that according to Isabelle there are five ghosts altogether." He wrote down '5 ghosts 'on the board. "That means that between us now we have met all five ghosts." He wrote down their names in order of the era in which they had lived in the house. "Fact number two they all returned here as ghosts and no matter how old they were when they died, they returned here as children. Michelle Victoria McGregor aged 10. Died much later but returned here as a 10-year-old ghost. Twins, Douglas and Calum McGregor aged 6. Died later at different times but both returned here as 6-year-old ghosts. Isabelle McGregor aged 14. Died later but returned here as a 14-year-old ghost". David McGregor aged 12. Died later but returned here as a 12-year-old ghost.

Michelle quickly interrupted her brother. "What about Isabelle's brothers? They never returned here when they died."

"Good point Michelle." Christopher praised his sister. "I wonder why they didn't. After all Vickie's little brother did. Remember he and his Nanny were seen by Michelle on our first day here."

"Yes, they must be here somewhere," agreed Nicholas. "You have to remember though that Isabelle's brothers were already adults and away from the house when she lived here." The others nodded and agreed that this explanation made sense.

Nicholas continued. "Fact number three and very importantly, what else do they all have in common?" He asked the others.

"They all have the same surname," Michelle shouted out.

"That's right. They are all McGregors. In fact, they are all members of our own family. Some are more distantly related than others, but the same clan never the less." Nicholas explained. "Fact four is that they all have another major thing in common. All their parents met the same fate." He wrote this down on the board.

Katie was one step ahead of her brother. Her brain went into overdrive. "Apart from the twins, the disappearances all occurred within the first year of moving into the house. In the twins' case, the second parent disappeared exactly one year to the date after the first parent." Katie was silent for a moment whilst she tried to get her thoughts in order. "Oh Crikes! Mum and Dad will disappear too and we will all end up as ghosts haunting this house too till the next unsuspecting McGregors come along and it will all happen again and again. That is what has happened to the others. That is what they are all trying to warn us about."

"Unless", Christopher interrupted his sister quickly, after glancing at his little sister and seeing the fear on her face. "Unless we can solve the mystery of what happened to all the other parents, before the anniversary of their disappearances. Don't you see? It's a pattern. The dates will all be the same. If we solve the mystery of what happened to them before that date, we save our parents and ourselves from the same fates. If not, we join them in that fate".

The room was silent as the children all tried to conquer their fears. To lose their beloved parents in such a way was unimaginable. To never know what had become of them was too horrid to even think about. It was suddenly all quite understandable just why the ghosts had all gathered back at the house at the time of their deaths. Each spirit was going back to that time in their lives which had shaped the rest of their living lives. They all had a deep-rooted need to know what had happened to the parents who were most dear to them. Their souls could not endure an eternity of not knowing. To know would free their spirits and give them peace, not only for themselves but for their parents too.

Katie was the first to recover. "We must find out the exact dates of the disappearances of all the parents."

"Yes." Christopher agreed. "That way we will know just how much time we have to solve the mystery."

Just then, in front of the children's astonished faces, a pen mysteriously and without any help from any one, lifted itself off the table, floated through the air and began to write on the whiteboard, all on its own. 'August 12'. The pen then dropped to the ground.

"Thank you, whoever you are." Michelle said quietly. "The ghosts are helping us," she told the others. "August 12. That is when the disappearances happened. Only one date was written down, so it is the same date for all of them." She told the others knowingly, before suddenly gasping. "*Oh no!* August 12 is tomorrow. We'll never solve it by then".

"What are we going to do? "Christopher moaned.

"Don't worry. We have one major advantage." Nicholas said confidently.

"What is that then Nick?" His brother asked.

"It's simple. We have been forewarned and forewarned is forearmed."

"What do you mean Nick? Talk sense not riddles". His confused little sister asked.

Nicholas attempted to explain. "We know what is expected to happen and why. We have the rest of today to solve why it happens and how it happens so that we can prevent it happening again, but if we don't manage to solve it by then, we can still gain ourselves some time. We can gain a whole year in fact. All we need to do is to make sure that Mum and Dad are away from home tomorrow night."

"Clever boy! That is brilliant!" Katie cheered. "There's only one problem. How do we get both Mum and Dad to go away tomorrow night? Never mind I'm sure between us we'll think of something if we must, but let's try to solve the mystery first."

Unfortunately, before the children could do anything further, their Mother called them to lunch. Chris quickly finished typing up the notes from the board into his laptop so that they would have a copy to keep and refer to. Michelle wiped the board clean when he finished, they quickly tidied away their things and went to wash up.

It was a very quiet lunch. Each child thinking about what they had learned that morning and trying to think of a way they could fix it all before tomorrow and if they couldn't they were thinking of ways in which they could get their parents to stay away for the night.

Mrs. McGregor wasn't used to seeing her children so quiet. Meal times were usually noisy affairs with all children talking and laughing at jokes or making plans. She was a little concerned but she had been assured by all of them that they were fine when she had tried to question them. She found it quite fascinating to watch them across the table. Their faces and expressions told a thousand words. She knew something was worrying them and that they were trying to solve something. Unfortunately, as she had been told many times by her children they were old enough to sort out their own problems and if they could not they would go to her. If only she knew just how big a problem they were wrestling with she might not have been so easy to let them get on with it.

The Ghost children were in their usual meeting place in the kitchen. "Well I think that went well, don't you?" Isabelle tried to be optimistic.

"At least they know now what will happen and how desperate their situation is." Agreed David. "Unfortunately knowing that and solving the mystery are two different things."

"Yes it is, but they are McGregors, and they are clever. With our help, there may be a chance." Vicky answered trying to remain optimistic.

"You cannae help them. You cannae tell them. You know the consequences if you do. Your souls will rot in purgatory if you do." A cheerful, gleeful voice piped up.

A boy suddenly appeared. He was sitting on a

window seat watching them.

“Go away Jamie! You haven’t won yet.” Calum and Douglas both shouted together.

“But I will.” Laughed Jamie as he floated away. “I will have my sweet revenge. I always do” The lights flickered on and off as his eerie laugh became louder before fading into the distance.

“I hope he is wrong this time. I really do” Douglas said softly. His friends nodded silently agreeing with him.

Chapter Nine

THE MISSING CLUE

As soon as lunch was over, the children quickly made their way back to the study. "Imagine Dad remembering about Isabelle." Michelle said.

"He didn't say that. Her sister corrected her. "He only said that he can vaguely remember his Dad talking about one of his uncles who had disappeared suddenly with his wife. He didn't know that it happened here though." It could have been Isabelle's parents or even the twins' parents."

During lunch, their parents, noticing how quiet and subdued their children looked had encouraged them to talk about their morning. Knowing that they could not tell them about the family curse, they had discussed the family history book. The children had told their parents about some of the interesting information that they had read about in the family history book.

They had not told them everything of course, only the relevant information, which if it became necessary, could be used to prepare the way to tell them everything. Grown-ups could be very skeptical about some things and to be believed they would need to be very convincing. They were afraid that in their Mothers delicate position it could prove to be too much of a shock if they did not prepare her for it beforehand.

The children were unsure what to do next. How could they solve the mystery if they didn't know just what they were looking for? Chris opened his laptop and brought up the file with all their clues and information. "Let's have another look at the facts," he suggested. " You never know it might help to go over everything again". The others agreed and it was whilst looking at this that Nicholas suddenly remembered something. He jumped up excitedly. "That's it!" He shouted. "The missing clue! I think I've found it!"

"Well don't keep it to yourself. Tell us." Christopher demanded exasperatedly, when it seemed that his brother was going to keep this news to himself.

"Okay. Listen. Isabelle told Katie that there were five of them. Between us we have met all five of them."

"So? What's your point Nick? We already know this". Katie asked him puzzled.

"Do you remember my first ghostly experience? When I was looking out of my bedroom window? Where do they all fit into the picture? Do you think that there could be a connection somewhere?" Nicholas asked the others anxiously.

"We forgot about that. Yes, of course. You must be right Nick. It's the only lead we have anyway." Christopher replied. "Can you still remember what happened? Tell us again."

Nicholas thought for a moment and then re-told them all about the night he had heard the horses' hooves and looked out his bedroom window to investigate the noise. He told them again about the stables and the blacksmith's forge where the blacksmith was busy shoeing a horse. He spoke again about the small boy helping the blacksmith and of their conversation in Gaelic, which he had overheard. He then told them once again about the woman he had seen. "The thing which I thought a little peculiar at the time was that although this was McGregor land, they were not wearing the McGregor tartan."

"Do you think that all this has something to do with them?" Michelle asked her brother. It was her sister who answered her question. "I'm sure they have to be part of it. Are you absolutely sure that it wasn't a McGregor tartan? Remember that there are several types of McGregor tartans, the dress tartan and the hunting tartan to name only two."

"I'm sure Sis. I know a McGregor tartan when I see one. I'm not sure which tartan this was but I do know that I would recognise it if I saw it again. They were talking about an Angus McGregor. They obviously did not like him. Maybe he is mentioned in the family history book. If he is, we might find out more about him. If we are lucky enough, it may even mention the blacksmith and his family."

All the time Nicholas was talking he was carrying out an internet search on his phone. He had googled Tartans and was scrolling through all the different types of clan tartans. Chris was on his lap top carrying out a search for any information on the farm. He had googled the name of the farm.

Katie found the old history book again and the girls were looking through the book. They found the page they were looking for. “Here it is!” Katie shouted. “It says that Angus McGregor was an unpopular landlord. The crofters resented him because he was not a Campbell. They blamed him for a potato famine. The book doesn’t say why. Now, wait a minute, this paragraph is interesting. It says here, that during the Highland Clearances, he was believed to have been responsible for burning to death a crofter and his wife.”

Hearing this, the boys stopped what they were doing and came across to hear more. They found out that it was the crofter’s son who blamed the Laird. The boy’s Father, Ewan Campbell did not like the new Laird, Angus McGregor. He worked as a blacksmith for Angus and in return he and his family were allowed to live in the croft. It was an arrangement that had been agreed by the old Laird Hamish McGregor When he died and his son Angus became owner, he began to clear the land to make way for the introduction of sheep into the area. There was more money to be made in sheep, and Angus, according to the book, was very interested in making money, the more the better.

When the potato famine occurred, Campbell automatically blamed it on Angus. It didn’t matter that the potato blight had affected all the crops in the country, he still blamed Angus. He began to make trouble with the other crofters. Angus put more pressure on Campbell to move out of the croft. Campbell refused to budge. When the croft was burnt down one night with Campbell and his wife still in it, Angus was blamed. The son managed to escape. There was no way that he could get justice done on behalf of his parents. The same thing was being done all over the Highlands. The law was on the side of the landowners not on the side of the poor crofters. What Jamie Campbell did, was to curse Angus McGregor and all those McGregors who would live in the house after him.

After Katie finished speaking, there was complete quietness in the room for several minutes whilst the children's minds digested this new information. "Wow! That's some book. It's told us everything we wanted to know so far. It's even better than the internet" Christopher was really impressed. "Who wrote it? "

"I'm not very sure. The name is not very clear. It's quite faded. I think it says Miss D. McGregor. I wonder how she knows so much." Katie asked puzzled.

"She'll probably be one of these people that collect history. What do you call them?" asked Michelle.

"An historian said Nicholas impatiently. "It ties in with the tartan I saw. I found it on the internet it is an old tartan belonging to the Campbells. Look!" He handed his phone round to show the picture of the tartan he had found.

"I found some interesting information about the house during my search too. Do you want to hear?" Christopher asked.

The others wanted to hear and Christopher told them that there were some newspaper reports about a man disappearing in the sixties. "It says that police are baffled over the man's disappearance exactly one year after his wife disappeared under exactly the same circumstances. It also says that it is not the first time that this has happened. During the war, a couple disappeared under suspicious circumstances. There are even people stating the house is haunted with some reports from people claiming to have seen ghosts. No wonder Dad got the house cheap with everyone thinking it was haunted. Ouch!" He shouted as his brother threw a cushion at him.

"It is haunted you dimwit! Don't you think that we are getting a little bit side tracked? Does this D. McGregor mention just exactly what this curse was, that this Jamie Campbell put on Angus? How did Jamie know for sure that it was Angus who set fire to the croft? Did he see him do it?"

Michelle laughed. "No silly. Angus was the boss; he would just have given orders to have it done. He wouldn't do the dirty jobs himself. Would he Katie?"

"No, you are quite right. He would've had a Factor in charge underneath him. Angus would have told him just what he wanted done. It would then be up to the Factor to carry out the Laird's wishes."

"Then surely that means that the Factor is the real culprit. He set fire to the croft." Christopher shouted triumphantly.

"Sorry to disappoint you, but it doesn't work that way. Technically speaking, yes, the Factor would be the one to start the fire, but he was only carrying out his orders. The guilty man is the man who gave the order to burn down the croft." Nicholas explained. "In this case it was Angus McGregor"

"Wait I don't understand. Just what is a Factor?" Michelle asked still a little puzzled. Nicholas explained patiently that a Factor was a sort of land agent or a foreman who would look after the land on behalf of the owner. The owner would tell the Factor what he wanted done and the Factor would make sure that the owner's wishes were carried out.

Christopher clapped his hands. "Good. Now that you know that can we get back to business? Do you think we can find out about this curse?" He asked impatiently. "There isn't much time."

"Okay down to business," Katie interrupted quickly as she saw Michelle's mouth begin to open in what would be the start of an argument with her brother. "This is what the book says about the curse. 'No McGregor should ever live happily in the house until the murderer of Ewan and Flora Campbell is brought face to face with his accuser. Until then all McGregor children should know exactly what it feels like to suffer the loss of their parents. When it happens, their soul should know no peace until such time that they can be reunited with their parents."

"Well that about sums it up, but the question is, now that we know, just what can we do about it?" Nicholas asked gloomily. "How can we stop it happening to us? Even if we were to find out the real murderer, it all happened such a long time ago, over a century ago. How on earth could we get them face to face? It's just impossible".

Michelle began to cry softly. "It's useless, isn't it? We are all doomed. I knew we should never have moved here." Katie however, was a great fan of ghost stories and was much more optimistic about everything than her younger sister was. "Oh, do stop being so pessimistic Michelle. It's not useless. Stop crying. Getting them face to face is the easy part. The difficult part is going to be trying to find out the person who really did burn down the croft." Michelle immediately stopped her crying and along with her two brothers stared at Katie. "How?" They chorused.

"Easy Peasy. We'll hold a séance." She told them. "The only problem is, we have to find out who did it first and we are running out of time."

"But surely it was our ancestor Angus McGregor who was responsible. He is the one who wanted them out so why would anyone else be responsible for their deaths?" Michelle asked. She was really puzzled now and having difficulty trying to understand her sister's logic.

Michelle's words made the children pause. They became quiet, each thinking the same dark thoughts. It was useless. As much as they hated the thought that their ancestor was a murderer, all the evidence pointed to the murderers being Angus and his factor. How could they accuse a member of their own family, dead or alive of being a cold-blooded murderer? It really was useless. They were all doomed.

Suddenly the atmosphere in the room changed. It

became warmer and there was an orange glow all around them. One by one the ghost children appeared in front of them. “Don’t give up! Stay strong!” Isabelle encouraged them smiling at them.
“Believe in us” the ghost twins said.
“Your quest for the truth is a just one.” Michelle Victoria stated. “Angus is not the murderer. We know this. You need to look elsewhere. You have the answer” Then suddenly they were gone and the room returned to normal.

Where moments before there had been an atmosphere of doom and gloom there was now a new feeling of optimism. Their ancestor was not a killer and they would prove his innocence. The ghost children were depending on their help and they would not, could not let them down. Somehow one way or another they would find out the truth and destroy the curse before their own parents were taken too.

“Do you think they will succeed?” David asked his friends.
“I hope so. I really hope so.” Vicky answered.
“They must succeed. They must for everyone’s sake. Theirs and ours.” Isabelle said firmly.
“They don’t have much time left.” Douglas gloomily reminded them.
The eerie laugh belonging to Jamie sounded above them. “Tomorrow.” His invisible voice taunted. “Tomorrow.

Chapter 10

MIDNIGHT MEETINGS

That night, the children gathered together in Michelle's bedroom. It had gone midnight and their parents were in bed asleep. They spoke in whispers so as not to disturb them. "Do you think that this will work?" Michelle whispered.

"I don't know but at this stage anything is worth a try." Nicholas replied. "You've heard the saying two heads are better than one? Well let's hope that in this case nine heads are better than one."

"What happens if they don't come?" Christopher asked.

"They will. In fact, they are probably here right now. They need to know answers as much as we do. Do you remember when the pen moved all by itself in the study?" Nicholas reminded them confidently. "Well that was them being helpful. They were in the study with us the whole time. All of them and I'll just bet that they are all here with us now. Aren't you?" he added slowly.

Although Nicholas was expecting the five friendly ghosts to appear, he was just as startled as his brother and sisters when the atmosphere in the room suddenly became warmer and took on a hazy, warm orangey mist. The children were not scared. How could they be when they could feel love all around them with the smell of roses and summer flowers. They were still startled though to see the orange mist form into bright glowing white orbs before manifesting into five human shapes. One by one the five ghostly children showed themselves.

When all five had made their presence known to the four living children, Michelle Victoria, acting as spokes ghost spoke up. "Yes, we were in the study too. We cannot help you further though. We are bound by the curse which will not allow us to help you. You must work out the answer for yourselves."

"If we had answers for you we would do everything in our power to help you, despite the curse." Isabelle added quietly and a little defiantly. "However, our knowledge is your knowledge." Isabelle added sadly. "Everything we know, you now know."

It was Michelle Victoria who after seeing the confused looks on the children's faces began to explain. "I was the first child to experience the force of the curse. My family was the first to suffer. I had never heard of the curse. It was only afterwards that I began to hear rumors. Through the years, I read all I could about the history of our family. Unfortunately, I never did solve the mystery and unfortunately no-one ever believed my theories about the house. At one stage, my Uncle talked about having me committed to an asylum for the insane. He believed that my grief over losing my parents was causing me to lose my mind. After that I gave up my search for the truth but I could never forget. Had I known I would revert back to myself as a child and return here as a ghost and other children would suffer as a result of my failure, I may have tried harder to make people believe me."

The twins Douglas and Calum took over the story. "We came across the history book before we met Michelle Victoria. Although we were both young, our Father was quite proud of the fact that we were extremely clever for our age." Douglas began.

"We first learnt to read at the age of four." Calum explained. "Anyway, we didn't really take much notice of the book and even after we met Michelle Victoria, we were both too young to make a difference to the eventual outcome."

Douglas continued sadly. "In our case we went through the agony twice. We tried to persuade our Father to move to a new house after the disappearance of our Mother, but he liked it here. He believed that our Mother would return to us and he wanted to be here waiting for her. He did not believe us when we tried to explain about the history book and about our having seen Michelle. We could not find the necessary proof to make him believe us as no adult can read the book. After his disappearance, we were sent away to live with our Grandparents who were our Mum's parents in Edinburgh. Neither of us imagined that we would end up back here."

It was now Isabelle who took over the story. "When I first came across the boys and Michelle Victoria, I was very frightened. I was more afraid of them than I was of the war going on in the world. I had never heard of the curse until I actually came across the book on my pillow one night." She laughed. "I would probably never have read it if Michelle Victoria had not frightened me into reading it." She looked across at the other ghost girl and they both smiled at each other at the memory. "Well actually she appeared and practically begged me to read it". She sighed. "I was never very bright and it took me too long to work out what it all meant. Afterwards, I tried to find out what I could but as you know I was sent to live with relatives in Clydebank. I had every intention of returning here after the war, once I was old enough, but unfortunately I never survived the war and I returned here anyway with my story added to the family history book." She sighed.

David began to talk. "I was twelve when I came to live in the house. In my case, just like you, we had not been here very long when my parents disappeared. We were only here a few weeks. The book practically followed me everywhere. It would appear on my bed, on the kitchen table, in the bathroom even, until one morning it fell from the air and hit me on the head. I gave up then and thought that if it wanted to be read that badly then I had better read it. Almost as soon as I had finished reading it the others visited me. It was too late to save my parents but when I moved down South, I found out through one of my Great, Great Uncles about the jealousy between Angus McGregor and his cousin's husband. Apparently, my Great, Great.

Uncle's Grandfather had been the brother of the cousin's husband and was in his confidence. I was traveling up here a few years later on my motor bike when I had my accident. I came so close to solving the mystery but only succeeded in adding my part to the family history book too." He finished, shaking his head regretfully.

Michelle Victoria once again began to talk. "So, you see my dears it is now up to you all to solve the mystery once and for all. What could be more fitting, after all I was the first victim of the curse. You are my direct descendants. The curse should end with you all."

"Yes, it could end with us", agreed Katie thoughtfully, "or we could end up adding to the family history book. I am right in thinking that you are all responsible for the book? It will continue to be added to until the mystery is solved, won't it?"

"Yes." Isabelle agreed," We must go now as the hour grows late. We wish you Good Luck. We will not see you again until it is over, one way or another. Take care. Our thoughts and prayers go with you. Good Luck! Good-bye."

One by one the ghost children made their farewells and then vanished as quickly and as silently as they had appeared. The atmosphere in the room returned to normal along with the wonderful flowery smell.

The children were quiet as they took in all their ghost relatives had said. Nicholas was the first one to recover. "Well, what do you think of all that? "

"We aren't any further forward, are we? I am too

tired to think just now." Christopher yawned.
"Yes, me too. We all are. I think we should go to bed now and hopefully tomorrow after a good night's rest we will feel refreshed enough to come up with answers." Katie said trying not to yawn too.
Michelle giggled. "You sounded just like Mum when you said that Katie. "I am off to bed. Night! Night!"
One by one the children quietly crept back to their rooms and quickly fell asleep.

The children were up early next morning. Chris was the first one awake. He had been restless. Something was niggling at him. He woke up suddenly knowing what it was. He went running into his brother's room and shook him awake. He had remembered a comment David had made the night before.

David had mentioned that he had found out something about their ancestor Angus McGregor. Perhaps this could be the missing piece of the puzzle. The clue they were looking for? After all David had said he had been very close to solving the mystery and lifting the curse. He explained all this to Nick and together they hurried to tell their sisters. The children rushed through their chores after breakfast and only an hour after getting up from bed they were once again gathered in the study. They were convinced that their answer would be found in the history book. It was. They found what they were looking for and were soon reading about the discovery that David must have made before his death.

Hamish Campbell was the husband of a younger

cousin to Angus McGregor. If Angus McGregor did not marry and produce his own heir, then the house with all the land would be inherited by Hamish. Hamish was even more ambitious than his cousin-in-law Angus. No one not even the Crofters who were members of his own Clan liked him. When Hamish heard rumors of Angus's intended marriage, he was furious. The land should be his. If the land had stayed with the Campbells he would have inherited it anyway as he had been next in the Campbell line to inherit. Once the land had been sold Hamish had tried to ensure that he would still own it by marrying the McGregor next in line to inherit. As her husband, he would automatically become the heir, as in those days, all the wife's possessions became the property of her husband. After hearing the news of the intended marriage, Hamish bribed Angus's Factor and was soon plotting with him to help him to kill his cousin - in - law. Ewan Campbell overheard the two men plotting and informed his wife. Now although there was no love lost between Angus and Ewan, as his Laird, Ewan did owe his loyalty to him. Unfortunately, before he could warn Angus, he and his wife were killed when their croft was burnt down. Hamish himself was murdered only a few days later. At the time, it was said that the murder had been the crofter's revenge against Angus in retaliation for Ewan and Flora Campbell's deaths. As they could not get close enough to Angus they retaliated by killing his heir.

Nicholas was the first to speak. "So let me get

this right." he went on. "So Hamish had the Factor murder Ewan and Flora, not Angus. Hamish must have discovered that Ewan had found out about the plot to kill Angus so he had them both murdered and set fire to the croft to cover the murders up. They were successful too." He added regretfully.
Christopher understood what his brother was saying "The Facto murdered the Campbells on orders from Hamish. It must have been he who murdered Hamish to prevent him telling on him. They must have fallen out over something".
"It doesn't matter what they fell out over. The point is, who is the real murderer? Is it the one who did the actual killing or the one who ordered the killing? Who do we bring Jamie Campbell face to face with?" Nicholas asked.
"Both of them". Michelle stated firmly. They are both equally just as guilty."
It was Katie's turn to frown then. "Yes. You are quite right, but we now have another problem and hardly any time to solve it. We need to know the Factor's name. In case you haven't noticed, we have now read the whole book and there has been no mention of the Factor's name."

The children were baffled. The one piece of vital information, which they most needed, was missing. They had succeeded in solving the mystery of who had murdered the Campbells, only to fail at the last hurdle. How could they bring the murderers face to face with their victims if they did not know the name of one of the murderers? "I don't suppose we could google it?" Michelle suggested hopefully.

"I doubt it." Katie replied. "Not everything can be found on the internet no matter what people say to the contrary. Never the less on the off-chance Christopher can you run a few searches?"
"Way ahead of you Sis", Christopher was already busy on his lap top but unfortunately after a few searches on several different search engines he found nothing.
"How about we try the library in town? Maybe they will have some old documents that might tell us his name." Christopher suggested.
"No not the library. Michelle Victoria checked the old library documents." Michelle reminded him.
"Yes, but that must have been many, many years ago now. Libraries update all the time." Christopher argued.
He had the agreement of the other two. Katie also had a suggestion to make. She thought that perhaps they would find the name in an old Parish register in the church.

To save some time it was decided to split into two groups. The boys would go to the library whilst the girls would go to the church and ask the Minister if they could have a look at the old Parish records of that time. That was if he still had any. As it was almost lunchtime they decided to go immediately after lunch.

Once the children left the study, the ghost children held their own meeting.

"They are so close now. Do you think they will make it in time?" Douglas asked.
"I hope so." David replied. They are finishing what I started and I was very close. Has anyone seen Jamie recently? Do you think he knows how close they are? Maybe he will allow them some extra time."
"You know as well as we all do that would be impossible. He is as much bound by the curse as we are. Once the curse is set in motion there is no going back. It has to be played out to the end, no matter what the consequences are." Victoria said sadly.
"We must try though," Isabelle tried to be positive, knowing that her friend was right. "Oh, where is that dreadful boy when we actually want to see him. Jamie come here we want to speak to you!" She shouted quite frustrated with the situation.

Chapter 11

TIME RUNS OUT

The girls were in luck. The Minister still had all the Parish records dated from even before the time they needed. He was delighted to show them to the girls. It was unusual to find such young people so interested in local history without having to be forced to learn it from teachers.

The Minister was so nice and so helpful that the girls were almost tempted to confide in him. Unfortunately, the curse stated that only McGregor children could bring the curse to an end. The Minister, Mr. Grieg was not even a McGregor. The girls did not dare risk involving him. Eventually, they found the name that they were looking for. They thanked the Minister for his time and patience with them then went off to meet the boys at the library.

The boys were already on their way to meet their sisters. They too had been lucky in their search for the missing name. The old village library had been moved to a brand new and updated library building only a few years ago and had obtained a copy of all the local parish documents. They were now kept in the reference department of the library.

"He was a Campbell too. Duncan Campbell". They all cried out together when they met up with each other. They laughed, and told each other how they had found out the name as they quickly walked home. They had all the facts now. It was like a jigsaw puzzle and now all the pieces had been fitted neatly into place. Now came the really scary task. Time was running out. It would be teatime soon. They had to hold a séance soon or it would be too late.

A shock was waiting for the foursome when they arrived home. The house was empty. A visit to the kitchen showed that the tea preparations had not been started. Perhaps their Mum had felt unwell and was having a lie down? Unfortunately, a search of her bedroom showed that it was empty. The children were really worried by this time. Had it happened already then? It couldn't have, surely it was much too soon. It was supposed to happen later, at night. Just as they were about to start panicking, the telephone began to ring. Startled, the children jumped, then all ran to answer the phone at the same time, Katie reached it first. She grabbed it and spoke breathlessly into the phone, praying for all she was worth that it would be one of her parents on the other end of the line. Her prayers were answered.

The phone call was from her Father. Their Aunt Winnie had made an unexpected visit to the house that afternoon and had persuaded their Mother to spend a few days with her at a spa resort in Aberdeen. He had driven them into the City to the Hotel. Their Father told them that he would be home soon and just to begin tea without him. He informed them that he had arranged with their neighbour, Mrs. Williams to come and stay with them until he arrived home. Katie on hearing this last piece of news had tried to persuade her Dad to stay overnight with their Mother but much to her disappointment, he insisted on coming home.

Mr. McGregor was shaking his head as he ended his phone call. Why was everyone determined to get him away from the Farm? He wondered. First it had been his wife's Aunt visiting very unexpectedly. Her visit had been so strange. She had arrived by Taxi, got out of the car and had just stood on the path just gazing up at the house with a strange look on her face and mumbling to herself. He had been looking out the window and so had noticed her arrival in the taxi and had gone to open the door to her. The door had stuck for no apparent reason. It had taken him a good five minutes before he could open the door. Then even stranger, she would not come in preferring to remain on the porch to explain the reason for her visit. She had then stated that the house would not welcome her in at this time. Very weird!

She wanted to treat both him and his wife to a couple of days at the spa resort. She had tried to persuade him by saying it would do them both good to relax and to spend time together on their own before the babies came. He had explained to her that much as he would like to it just wasn't possible as he was very busy on the farm at the moment. He could tell she was not very pleased that he would not be persuaded. She had practically begged him and had said she would watch the children. He shook his head again. It was all very weird. His wife had been very eager to spend time with her Aunt and had quickly gone to pack a case. They had left very soon afterwards.

Just as Katie had finished explaining the situation to her brothers and sister, a knock was heard at the front door. Mrs. Williams had arrived. They had no chance of holding the séance now until she was gone. Mrs. Williams was a kind but nosy neighbour. Christopher sighed. "Oh well, at least we'll only have Dad to worry about to-night. Mum is quite safe with Aunt Winnie."

Mr. McGregor arrived home about 9.30 p.m. It took a further half an hour before their neighbour decided to go home. The children had made some plans whilst their Father had been gone. The three older children would hold the séance in the study whilst Michelle, being the youngest and not at all eager to join in, would have the very important task of keeping an eye on their Father.

It was easy to get her Dad's attention and to keep it focused on herself whilst the other three slipped quietly to the study. Mr. McGregor had already begun to teach his youngest daughter the basic moves of chess. He had been amazed at how quickly she had picked up the rules of the game. Now she appeared eager for another lesson.

In the library, preparations for the séance were in progress. Both Katie and Nicholas had heard from some older friends just what to do and Chris had done his thing by carrying out a search on the internet on how to hold a séance step by step. It was amazing what you could find on You Tube, he thought. Nicholas had sneaked upstairs earlier and had already written out on some small cut out squares the letters of the alphabet, the words yes, no, man, woman and numbers 0-9. Katie had brought a small glass from the kitchen. They placed the squares in a large circle with the glass upside down in the centre of the circle. “According to the video on You Tube, this is the right way to do it.” Christopher said a little worriedly. “You know as well as I do that Mum disapproves of this sort of game. She says that messing about with things that we know nothing about can be dangerous. She says we mustn’t meddle with anything we know nothing about We can be opening ourselves up to really wicked, dangerous and harmful things”

“I know what Mum says and that we shouldn’t do this. I know that it can be dangerous but we are not playing a game here. Lives depend on us getting this right, so just this once let’s just hope and pray that it does work. If Mum knew the reasons she would forgive us. Okay?" Nicholas said, justifying their actions.

“If Mum knew the reason we would all be out this house so fast our feet wouldn’t touch the ground” Katie reminded them both.

They would never ordinarily do this especially as their Mother had expressly forbidden any kind of game like this, but this was not an ordinary time as he had already pointed out. “It’s almost 10.30 p.m. Let’s begin. Put one finger on the glass and whatever happens *do not* take it off again and *do not* push the glass. Keep the other hand flat down on the table. Okay?”

Just as they were about to begin, Michelle began to shout from the other room. "Katie, Nick, Chris. Come quick. Dad's acting weird. Come quickly". She sounded very frightened. The others immediately stopped what they were doing and ran to join her.

She was standing blocking the entrance to the front door, tears streaming down her face, trying to prevent her Father opening the door. He seemed to be in some kind of trance. He was not even aware of their resistance. Before the others could stop him, he had lifted Michelle away from the door, opened it and walked out of the house. "Quick, follow him. We'll find out where he goes. It will be where all the other parents are probably. Quickly! We mustn't let him out of our sight." Nick whispered urgently.

Mr. McGregor led them through the garden, past the outbuildings and onwards, till he came to the clump of trees which his daughter had found on her first day at the house. He came out of the trees into the clearing beside the pond. "They can't be in the pond. It isn't deep enough" Michelle whispered. "No but there is an old disused and very deep well just in amongst those trees over there." Christopher pointed. "I came across it a few days ago. Quickly, we have to get him out of that trance before he reaches it. He'll fling himself down it if we don't stop him."

Frantically the children tried to bring their Dad out of the trance. He was in a deep, deep trance and took no notice whatsoever of them. He was on the other side of the pond now heading through the trees towards the old well. The atmosphere felt very strange the closer they came to the well. It was suddenly very dark with a strange swirly clammy cold mist all around them making the children very cold and frightened.

There was a ghostly figure waiting by the well. As they moved closer to the well, Nicholas suddenly recognised the figure. He looked just the same as when Nicholas had seen him that night outside his bedroom window apart from the evil smirk of satisfaction on his face now. "It's Jamie Campbell!" He shouted. "He wants his revenge!" Without stopping to think, Nicholas ran in front of his Father. The other children seeing him do this did the same. "Leave him alone Jamie Campbell. He is not the one you want." He shouted. "You are taking revenge against the wrong people. The McGregors did not murder your parents. Return our Father to us and I promise you that before this night is over you will be face to face with the people who really did murder them." Nicholas crossed his fingers behind his back and silently recited a short pleaful prayer.

Jamie Campbell just stared hard at Nicholas who stared right back at him. Nicholas knew that he could not afford to act scared or back down in any way. Eventually Jamie nodded. "You've got till this night is done. If you dinnae gae me whit I want, it will be you I'll tak". In the next instant, he was gone. The strange atmosphere lifted and their surroundings appeared normal again.

As soon as he had disappeared, Mr. McGregor was shaking his head and blinking. "What on earth happened?" He noticed his children. "What is going on? Don't try telling me nothing," he warned them. "I may not have been able to anything about it but I heard and saw all. Was that boy really what I think he was or was it one of your friends dressed up playing a weird sort of joke"? He asked hopefully. "On second thoughts let's go back indoors. I've a feeling that I am going to have to be sitting down to hear this explanation."

Once they were all back inside, he was told the whole story. Knowing that his children would never lie to him, he sat shaking his head. "If I had not seen him with my own eyes, I would never have believed you. You have coped with this all on your own? Why on earth did one of you not tell me what was going on?"

"Would you have believed us?" Nicholas asked.

His Father sighed. "No, probably not. Well I know now, so what do we do now?" He asked his children.

The children looked at one another. Their Father was an adult and as much as it would be a relief to have a grown up take charge, they were not supposed to involve adults. Mr. McGregor saw the looks exchanged between his children. "No! Don't even think about excluding me now!" He said firmly and very determinedly. "I am involved now and I am a McGregor. This same thing could have happened when I was a child. There is no way that I am going to allow you all to take part in a séance, which could prove dangerous. At least not without having me present." He stated very firmly.

His children heaved big sighs of relief. They had no option but to agree. Now Dad would bear the responsibility. They told him so and he admitted that although he had never taken part in a séance before, he would do his best. He made them all promise that on no account would anyone inform their Mother about the night's events. She would only worry needlessly and she would want them all to move. They were all sworn to secrecy. Their Mother would never know just how close their family had come to disaster, at least not if they could prevent it.

Whilst all this was going on the unseen ghost children silently watched. They did not require their voices to speak to each other. They could communicate telepathically between themselves. Calum was worried. "It's not aloud. He can't interfere. If he does he will bring on the wrath of the curse and we will all end up in purgatory. Stop them Michelle!" He pleaded.

"Shh! don't worry! Everything is fine". Michelle Victoria soothingly reassured him. Don't you see? It was Jamie himself who involved the children's father. By granting the children extra time to prove the family's innocence and breaking his hold on the father he has unwittingly broken that part of the curse so it no longer applies."

"Does that mean we can help them too now?" David asked.

"Unfortunately, No I do not think so. We must content ourselves with watching from the shadows for now. But you know I really am hopeful that everything is going to turn out just fine." Michelle Victoria smiled as they all floated into the next room.

Chapter 12

THE SÉANCE

It was just after midnight when the séance finally began. All four children and their Father sat around the round table, which Mr. McGregor had brought through from the dining room. With her father now present and sitting beside her Michelle had decided that she was now brave enough to take part in the séance. This time round they all held hands to form a circle. The glass still in the middle of the ring of letters they finally began.

Mr. McGregor did all the talking. He was unsure how one went about contacting a particular spirit. His son Christopher had given him the step by step instructions on how to hold a séance to read, which he had printed from the internet earlier. His children never ceased to amaze him. He began by saying his name and explaining who he was. He then said that he needed to contact someone in the spirit world and asked if there was anyone there who could help him.

Michelle's skin became quite cold and her arms were all goose bumps. She was shivering. She knew something was about to happen. She had felt the same way earlier at the well when Jamie Campbell had first appeared.

Suddenly the glass began to move. Michelle almost began to scream but bit down into her bottom lip instead. They had been warned to keep very quiet during the proceedings. The glass circled the letters twice before stopping in front of the word *'yes'*. Mr. McGregor thanked the spirit for helping and asked if the spirit was a man or a woman. The glass circled the letters again before coming to a stop beside the word *'man'*. "What is your name?" Was Mr. McGregor's next question to the spirit.

The children gasped when the glass finally finished spelling out his name. The spirit was none other than Angus McGregor himself. No wonder he wanted to help them, after all he was the man who had been blamed for the murders. He wanted to clear his name and prevent the curse happening to any more of his family. Mr. McGregor then asked Angus if he could contact the two spirits he was looking for, Hamish Campbell and Duncan Campbell.

Everyone held their breaths. Would Angus find them? After a few minutes of silence and calmness, the room suddenly became very cold, although the central heating had been switched on. The light flickered a few times but luckily, remained on though it was not quite as bright as it had been. The glass beneath their fingertips suddenly went crazy. It circled the letters a few times going faster and faster before losing control completely and flying off the table to smash on the floor.

Michelle bit even deeper into her lip. She was terrified. Katie could not help herself and let out a scream. Mr. McGregor quickly tightened his hold on her hand and whispered "Shh! It's all right". His two sons had gone very pale but remained quiet.

Footsteps and loud whispering could be heard in the room above. Doors banged so loudly the furniture in the room began to shake. The chandelier in the room was swinging furiously backwards and forwards so much so that Mr. McGregor fully expected it to fall down and break. The children were absolutely terrified. The loud whispering had now become loud voices arguing in Gaelic and then the banging became even louder. Footsteps were now heard stamping down the stairs.

Suddenly the study door was thrown open and an icy cold mist and roaring wind blew all around them. The children sat too petrified to move. Their Father too was very scared though afterwards he would not admit that to anyone. The children could now see weird shadows on the wall. The lights were flickering madly which gave the shadows the appearance of grotesque menacing monsters. The whole atmosphere was very creepy and sinister. The shadow figures manifested into wispy see through apparitions before finally turning into solid figures and took on the shapes of men who were unwillingly being manhandled into the room.

More figures began to appear in the room. All the figures were dressed in eighteenth century clothing. The first two figures who had been forcibly brought to the room both wore the same tartan, though the younger man's clothing seemed to be of a better quality. The older man's clothes made it known that he was underneath the younger mans' social status. That meant that he had to be Duncan

Campbell the Factor, Christopher thought correctly. He was terrified but fascinated by this turn of events. What would happen next, he wondered? Hamish and Duncan had been escorted by several fierce looking ghosts all wearing the McGregor tartan. One actually smiled at Michelle and winked.

Two more figures appeared. One was Jamie Campbell; another was obviously Angus McGregor. He looked so much like the children's own father that he just had to be their ancestor. The figures began to speak. "Cò dares a 'cuimhneachadh dhuinn seo bàsmhor àite?" ("Who dares to recall us to this mortal place?") Hamish asked very indignantly in Gaelic. "Carson a tha sinn air a thoirt an seo?" ("Why have we been brought here?") "Dè that hu ag iarraidh?" ("What do you want?") He looked around the room turning a very intimidating eye around the table staring at them one by one till finally fixing his gaze on Mr. McGregor. Before Mr. McGregor could begin to speak, his elder son stood up fearlessly and faced the spirit. "*We* dare recall you". Nicholas began quickly before his nerve failed him. "*You*, Hamish Campbell and you also, Duncan Campbell have escaped justice for too long whilst other innocent people have been punished and made to suffer for crimes which *you both committed.*"

He paused and Katie took over "Yes". She agreed. "You Hamish Campbell plotted to kill your cousin-in- law, Angus McGregor. Through your own greed and jealousy of him, you plotted with Duncan Campbell". She turned and pointed an accusing finger, first at Hamish and then at Duncan. "You were overheard by the blacksmith, Ewan Campbell, so to prevent him warning Angus McGregor, both of you cruelly and cold bloodedly murdered Ewan and then his wife who was a witness to your crime."

Christopher now took over. "You both set fire to the croft to cover up your crime and to make it look as if Angus was the person responsible. You, Duncan Campbell then made your crime worse by telling Jamie Campbell that you were acting under Angus McGregor's orders and that it had been Angus himself who had set fire to the croft."

Not to be left out although with a very shaky voice, Michelle then took over from Christopher. "You then murdered Hamish Campbell so that no-one would find out what you had done. It is because of you that our family has been cursed." She sat down with a thump, her shaky legs too weak to support her any longer. She stopped talking. The ghosts were now arguing so loudly she would not have been heard anyway. Hamish and Duncan were not happy at being exposed for their crimes. They were fighting with their captors and trying to get away from them. Hamish Campbell managed to escape briefly before Angus recaptured him.

During his brief moment of freedom, he flew around the room, causing a very cold icy wind. The room temperature dropped several degrees causing the children to see their breaths. Nicholas felt his icy cold touch as the evil spirit squeezed his arm so tightly it left marks on his upper arm.

Nicholas gasped in pain. Hamish looked him straight in the eyes and Nicholas shivered. This ghost hated him and wanted to do him harm. Hamish laughed an eerie wicked cruel laugh. Nicholas felt the icy cold ghostly fingers move from his arm to his throat and around his neck. This ghost meant to kill him. He had the insane thought in his head imagine being killed by a ghost. In the background, there was pandemonium. His sisters were screaming. His brother and his father were shouting and trying to get close enough to help him but they could not move out their chairs. Some unseen force was keeping them glued to their seats. Nicholas could not see what was going on but he could hear that Duncan Campbell too had managed to escape his captors.

Suddenly the room temperature changed again. It took on an orange glow and became increasingly hotter. The children could smell burning. The room was on fire! Embers from the burning roof began to rain down on them. They could smell burning flesh. It was horrific. The girls were screaming. They were all going to be burned alive. Mr. McGregor tried to protect his children. He stood up and shouted very loudly "STOP IT!" He was ignored. He felt himself being pushed back down into his chair by some unknown force and a ghostly hand put over his mouth. Just as Nicholas was resigning himself to their impending death Angus and his men managed to recapture the evil spirits and Nicholas was free. "STAD A CHUR AIR" ("STOP") ENOUGH!" Angus was absolutely furious with Hamish. He was so mad he shook him like a rag doll. “How dare you hurt this boy. He is my kin. You have wronged my family enough and you dare add to your sins?” He roared. Finally, the ghosts were brought under control. The room suddenly came back to normal. No fire and no terrible smell.

In her head Michelle could hear very loudly and clearly “DO NOT BREAK THE CIRCLE!” It was her Aunt Winnie’s voice. Michelle smiled. She didn’t know how but she knew her aunt must have used her psychic powers to communicate with her. She was about to tell the others but Chris beat her to it. “We must not break the circle.” Chris said with a surprised look on his face. He had heard his Aunt’s voice too. He looked across at his little sister and smiled managing to give the thumbs up sign and mouthed “Everything is going to be okay now.” Michelle smiled back. She knew her brother who had never before shown any psychic abilities had also heard her Aunt’s voice.

Nicholas who seconds before had been very shaken up was now calmer. Everything had happened so quickly. His father was urgently asking him if he was all right. They still could not move from their chairs but Nicholas could. He nodded. He had to see this through to the end. He knew what had to be done and the voice in his ear was telling him to have courage!

Katie was still in a panic and remained too traumatised to hear any voice in her head. Everything had looked and felt very real. There still looked to be burn marks on the back of her hand

and arm where some of the embers had landed on her. She had been so terrified during the ordeal that nothing could have got through to her. Now however with everything under control she was realizing that it had not been real. Just an illusion conjured up by the evil spirits into scaring them. She too now could hear her Aunt's voice trying to reach out to her. "Katie! Calm down! It isn't real! They were trying to scare you into breaking the circle. You must calm down! Do you hear me? Everything is going to be all right. Trust yourself, trust your sister and brothers. Please listen to me. Hear my voice." The voice in her ear tried to reassure her. Katie was much calmer now that she knew no one was trying to kill and burn alive her family. "Yes, Aunt Winnie I hear you." She whispered. "I am calm now. Thank you." She smiled.

The ghosts were puzzled when they saw the children smile at each other. They had used up most of their energy trying to scare these children into breaking the circle which was keeping them in this world. Now there would be no escaping from their crimes.

Nicholas coughed and cleared his throat, took a deep breath and stood up. He turned to Jamie Campbell now. His throat felt a little sore and dry. In a raspy voice he began to speak. "We have brought you face to face with your parents' murderers now. You can rest in peace now that the true story is known and you know their identities. You wrongly accused and cursed my family. We have proved to you that our family was innocent of any crime against your family. We ask that you now release us from the curse you put on us."

"Aye that you have done." Jamie agreed. "You have proved to me that I was wrong. I am very sorry that because of the lies I was told by a member of my own clan." He looked across at Hamish and Duncan looking for any signs of remorse and regret but all he saw was contempt and hatred. He sighed. "I too wronged your family. I cannae undo what has already been done but I can release the curse from your family. From now on McGregors may live in peace in this house. You have nothing to fear from me, and if I can prevent it, from my kin any longer." Once again, he looked across at the two men. He feared that this family had not heard the last from his kinsmen. "I am truly sorry but they have vowed to get even with you all for exposing them."

Angus spoke. "We will watch them carefully to keep them from causing mischief for you. Thank you all for clearing our family name. I am very proud to call you all my Kin." He smiled warmly at them as he and his men with Hamish and Duncan vanished in a wisp of smoke.

"I thank you all for allowing me finally to join my parents to rest in peace." Jamie smiled at them all and then just as suddenly he too was gone.

The lights grew brighter and the room quickly warmed up once again. It was finally over. Justice had been done and the curse had been lifted so that the McGregor family could now live in peace.

The children were left visibly shaken but glad that it was all over. After making sure that his children were all safe he examined his son's arm. It was red, swollen and bruised but he would survive. Whilst the children tidied up the room, their Dad made them all hot milky drinks. He put a generous amount of honey into Nicholas's milk to help soothe his sore throat caused by the ghost trying to strangle him. It was almost morning when everyone finally went to bed. The girls shared Katie's room whilst the boys shared Christopher's room.

Chapter 13

AUNT WINNIE

Meanwhile in an Aberdeen hotel suite, the children's Aunt Winnie was relaxing with a large glass of wine. The day had been both stressful and eventful. Winnie felt both physically and emotionally drained.

Although one of the world's strongest psychics, even she had had her doubts as to whether or not she could pull off what she just had. She had known that her skills and abilities alone would not be enough to help her great nieces and nephews succeed in their dangerous quest for truth. Summoning ghosts in the spirit world in order to answer for their past crimes in the mortal world was not an easy or safe thing to do. It could all have gone drastically wrong with fatal results for them all including herself. The ghosts could have been too powerful, which would have resulted in her being over powered and her spirit being taken back to the spirit world. This would leave her physical body as a vacant shell for some other spirit to jump into and inhabit it for them self.

She sighed. Another problem could have been if she had not managed to link with the children. She would have been unable to help them, to give them the strength and encouragement, they needed to gain their courage and succeed over the ghosts.

Winnie took a sip of her wine. She was so glad

that everything had gone in their favour. She was so thankful that over the years she had learnt to pay attention to her dreams and watch for any signs in them, which would assist her in her life. For the past few months her dreams had been predicting a fight of the spiritual kind. To begin with, Winnie hadn't really known what the dreams meant. She had believed that maybe the dreams were predicting a change in the direction of her psychic work. When the invitation came to set up and teach a new psychic training programme in Greece, she had thought that this was what her dreams had been about. However the dreams had not stopped, instead they had become more frequent and more urgent. When she had spoken with the children whist they were on holiday in Fife a couple of weeks ago, the dreams had suddenly become clearer and even more urgent.

When Winnie had received the message from her niece Mary, everything had become clear and she had known what she had to do. She had arranged for another gifted psychic to take over the position in Greece and had begun her preparations.

Linking with her spirit guides during her daily meditation session, she had asked for clarity and guidance. With their help she had gone to the farmhouse to try to find out the problem. Imagine her surprise and shock when she could not even enter the house. The spirits living in the house had sensed her power and had forbidden her entry into the house. The message was loud and clear. Do NOT INTERFERE. At first Winnie had felt frustrated and a little angry, but knowing this would not get her any answers, she had quickly calmed down. She asked for help from her spirit guides. A few moments later a figure appeared by her side. It was the old Nursemaid. This was the loophole no one had thought of. The old nursemaid was not a family member. She was not bound by the rules of the curse. She had remained in the house because she chose to be there. She had her own reasons for choosing to remain earth bound.

The Nursemaid did not speak directly to Winnie, instead she communicated through one of her spirit guides. When Winnie found out the extent of the danger her family was in she was horrified. She had to think quickly about the best way forward.

Getting her niece away from the house and to go with her was the easiest part. Unfortunately, her nephew – in - law proved to be stubborn. He would not leave the property. Winnie's hands were tied. She could not tell him about the curse. Everyone would have been in terrible danger if she did. He did agree to take them to the station. Winnie would have liked to have seen the children but they were nowhere to be seen, so reluctantly had to leave without reassuring them that she would be here for them.

After arriving back at the hotel and over a cup of tea and jam scones, Mary McGregor had told her Aunt about her ghostly experiences and her suspicions. Winnie had reluctantly confirmed her suspicions and had informed her of everything else she had since found out. After calming her very alarmed niece, she quickly reassured her that she had a plan to help the children and remove the curse. Winnie also explained that she could not do it on her own. She told her niece that she required the help from another gifted psychic. She needed assistance from her niece. Now was the time for Mary to use the psychic gifts she had been born with. Mary was a little surprised to hear her Aunt call her gifted and needing her help. She had always known she had gifts but had never wanted to use them. However this was urgent. Her family was involved and she would do all that was necessary to keep them safe.

Winnie lit a large lemon aromatherapy candle and placed it in the middle of a small round table. The lemon candle would promote clarity and enhance their psychic powers and help them contact the spirits.

Next Winnie went to her collection of crystal stones and selected a few. Each crystal held a different energy power. Amethyst to use against psychic attacks, and help open communication with spirit guides. It would also help with her telepathy and psychic abilities. Clear Fluorite to protect psychically by guarding against psychic attacks and to strengthen consciousness. Winnie then selected a Honey Calcite stone which would enhance her psychic abilities and aid in her astral projection and higher consciousness. After another rummage through the crystals Winnie brought out a chunk of Iolite. This was a very strong shaman stone. It was used to stimulate visions. Winnie had used it this way in the past but this time she was using it to expand her psychic talents. She then brought out another shaman stone. This time it was Labradorite. This stone would bring grounding to Winnie on her astral travel. It would keep her spirit connected to the physical world whilst it was away in another place. Winnie intended using astral travel to be where the children were. She would then use her telepathic ability to connect telepathically with their minds and try to give help and guidance when they were engaged with the spirits in a battle for the truth. Winnie was in no doubt that there would be a battle and that the children would be pushed to their limits.

She was worried too. Her plan depended on linking with the children's minds telepathically. She knew for sure that her great niece Michelle, was aware of being psychic, but the others had as yet not recognized their own psychic abilities. Winnie had known since their births that all four children would be born gifted. She had been prepared to wait till they had realised their psychic abilities in their own time. However this had changed things. Now there was no choice and she would have to try to somehow unlock their minds and make them become aware of their psychic powers within. Only then would they be strong enough to do battle with the spirits and finish victorious.

Winnie looked through her crystals for one last stone. She brought out an amulet made of black kyanite attached to a black lace. She explained to her niece that the black kyanite was used to channel the spirits. It provided protection and deflected negativity. She held the amulet in her left hand and covered it with her right hand. She closed her eyes and recited a short prayer of protection and love then fastened the necklace around Mary's neck. This would now form a strong protective shield around mother and babies.

Once the candles were lit and placed on the table, Winnie and Mary sat on opposite sides and held hands. Together they concentrated their energies on calling on their spiritual guides to help them bond together and form the psychic link to help them in the coming battle. It was very powerful, Winnie had known her niece was gifted but had been unaware of just how powerful a psychic she really was. With the combined energies of both their spirit guides and their own energies, Winnie felt so powerful that it was a little difficult to remain grounded. She touched the Labradorite crystal and quietly recited a short prayer asking the power of the stone to protect and keep her grounded.

Winnie's plan was to use her psychic powers to astrally project her spirit back to the farmhouse so she could see and hear what was taking place. She would use her powers of telepathy to link with the children and offer help and strength if needed.

Luckily her plan had worked, although it had not been without difficulty. After a particularly hard kick in the side from one of the babies, Mary had broken concentration and Winnie had felt herself being pulled back to the hotel room. It had been during that lapse in concentration that the spirits had broken free and caused their chaos. Fortunately Mary had quickly regained concentration and Winnie had been on hand to help and support the children to overcome their fears and take back control of the situation.

Winnie sighed and took a long sip of her wine. She was so proud of all of her great nieces and nephews. She was worried though that their ordeal would have some future consequences, such as nightmares. Even more worryingly was her certainty that this would not be the last time that the children would require her help. Whilst in the farmhouse in her spirit form, she had sensed other spirits in the background watching. Not part of the proceedings but watching very carefully. Winnie knew there was more to come but she had no idea what form it would take.

Her mind made up, she decided that she would move her school closer to the farm where she would teach all four children in psychic development. In the immediate future she would invite herself for a long stay at the farm. Her mind made up Winnie finished her wine, tidied up and went to bed.

Chapter 14

NEW BEGINNINGS

By the time the children woke and arrived downstairs for a very late breakfast next morning, their Father had already made a few phone calls. He had arranged for the old well to be investigated. He was so sure that the skeletons of the other missing McGregors would be found there that he had already arranged with the Minister to perform a proper burial in the church graveyard for them.

A few days later all this had been carried out. The children had just arrived home from the church service and were sitting in the study talking. "Do you think that Vicki and the others are at peace now?" Michelle asked.

"Yes. I hope so anyway." Her sister replied. She picked up the history book, which was still lying on the table. As she picked it up the room took on a warm bright orange glow and five ghost children appeared.

They were smiling and looked happy. "We just wanted to thank you all and to say our good-byes." Isabelle explained. "Without your help, we would not have been reunited at long last with our beloved parents. We are finally at peace. We were growing so weary of it all and when you all came to live in the house we grew hopeful again. Now thanks to you all, your Aunt and your Father we are weary no longer." She took the history book from Katie.

Michelle Victoria spoke now "Thank you my dears. I am proud that you are my descendants. A part of me lives in you all. Have a good life. She moved closer to Michelle and whispered in her ear. "Look in your jewelry box my dear! I have left you a special present." She smiled. "Our parents are beckoning to us so we must go now. Good-bye." They smiled, waved their good-byes and were gone before the children could even blink.

Michelle ran up the stairs to her room straight to her jewelry box and quickly opened it. Inside nestling against the velvet interior sat a small Victorian brooch. It was the cameo brooch belonging to the other Michelle. It was the brooch which had begun their ghostly adventures. Michelle mouthed a silent "Thank you" and she could have sworn she heard a very faint "You are very welcome". She smiled and ran back downstairs to show the others.

The whole episode was now completely over. The room was back to normal. The book too had gone. Life could now get back to normal again, or could it?

A few days after their last encounter with their ghost friends, the McGregor children were busy cleaning out one of the out buildings on the farm. Their Father, trying to take their minds away from the events of the past few weeks had given them one of the small empty sheds, which was quite close to the house to use as a games room. The deal he had made with them was if they took over the job of clearing out the shed and giving it a thorough clean, he would arrange for electricity to be installed and for it to be painted. He would then install a television with a sky movie package, a computer, games console with some games for them all. The children could then have the games room to themselves.

Three of his children thought that this was a great idea and began work in the shed immediately. Katie had needed some persuading to join in. She was uneasy and did not really like the shed. Her father put her reluctance down to the recent events and eventually had persuaded his daughter that there was nothing to fear.

It was hard dirty work but they didn't mind. The end result would be worth all the effort. The quicker they finished their part of the deal then the quicker their Dad could complete his part. The children worked well as a team and finally the shed was empty of all its old rubbish. After a short break, they would begin cleaning it.

However, before they could begin on the cleaning, the girls were sent on a short errand for their Mother, who had now returned home, so the boys were starting the cleaning on their own. When the girls arrived to start work, the boys were mumbling away excitedly to each other. "Come on. We are supposed to be cleaning up you two. Don't think you're going to leave it all for Michelle and I to do." Katie moaned angrily to her brothers.

As she walked slowly and a little hesitatingly into the shed, she could see that the old wooden stool and chair, which had been flung out with the rest of the rubbish, were once again back in the shed. She turned angrily towards the two boys. "What did you put them back in for? We were meant to be clearing the rubbish out, not keeping it."

"We didn't put them in". Christopher denied.

"Then who did?" Michelle asked.

"They did. " Nicholas told them, pointing towards the chair and stool.

Sitting on the stool was a small boy who looked about eight years old. On the chair was a small girl who looked only a year or two older than the boy was. Both were very poorly dressed in what looked like it might have been seventeenth century clothing. "Oh gosh! Are they ghosts? " Michelle gasped in surprise.

"I'm afraid so". Nicholas answered laughing.

"Oh no here we go again" Michelle groaned laughing with her brothers. No one noticed Katie's horrified gasp as she ran from the shed. Nor did they notice the look of recognition which passed between the two ghost children. They were too busy laughing and already looking forward to their next adventure.

The End

Note from Author

Hi I hope you enjoyed my first book in 'The Hauntings of Thistlebrae Farm' series.
I would love to know what you thought of it. You can email me at Rosieann.Stewart@yahoo.co.uk

Coming Soon!

Past Lives

Join the McGregor children in a new ghostly adventure.
Why does Katie hate the barn so much?
Why is Katie so frightened of the two little ghost children and what do they know that she doesn't?
Exactly who are they and will Katie survive finding out?

www.ingramcontent.com/pod-product-compliance
Lightning Source LLC
LaVergne TN
LVHW051004080826
845145LV00009B/2457

* 9 7 8 1 9 1 6 0 8 5 7 1 8 *